KRAKEN ISLAND

ERIC S. BROWN

SEVERED PRESS
HOBART TASMANIA

KRAKEN ISLAND

ISBN: 978-1-925493-25-2

KRAKEN ISLAND

An utterly inhuman shriek rang out in the jungle. Others followed it. All of them grew closer with each passing second as Corporal Davis ran. His knuckles were white from the tightness of the grip he clutched his rifle in. His legs pumped beneath him as his breath came in ragged gasps. Sweat slicked his sunbaked skin and seeped from the hair covered by his combat helmet to run into his eyes, burning them. He blinked away the sweat, continuing to push himself to his limits. Every muscle in his body ached, but he knew that if he slowed, even in the slightest, he was dead. He was the only one left. His entire unit was dead. Davis was doing his all-out best not to join them.

They had come to this island expecting a fight, knowing that they were outnumbered before their boots ever touched its soil. Those things were just part of the job. His unit had faced far worse odds than the intel report had laid out for them here and emerged victoriously. They were the best of the best. It was as simple as that. For the last two years, they had traveled the globe, their way paid by Uncle Sam, taking out the threats that folks back home didn't even want to know existed. They had cut their way across the Middle East like a blade sliding into the stomach of a terrorist.

When the details of this operation had landed on Colonel Jones' desk, the old man had almost told the higher ups to go to Hell or at least that was how the rumors went. Quite a few in the unit liked to talk about the old man and his hunches. He had led them all through Hell and back so many times, his hunches were like the word of God to them. If the old man suspected trouble or things to fall apart, you could bet they would. No one was quite sure why he had such a feeling on this one though. The operation looked on paper just like any other op they had run before. Get in, eliminate the enemy, and get out before anyone that mattered knew they were there.

The old man had been right too. Things had gone to Hell almost from the very moment they hit the island. The enemy they had been expecting wasn't the enemy that was waiting on them. Their advantage of surprise was gone, and they were the ones who were completely blindsided. They were hit while they were still trying to figure out what was going on and paid the price troops usually do when they are handed bad intel to guide them.

It wasn't so much a fight as a massacre. Davis had only escaped because, for the first time in all his years of service, he had run when the crap hit the fan. And he was still running now.

Corporal Davis never saw the piece of vine on the jungle floor that caught his ankle as he plowed headlong through the trees. One instant, he was running full out, and the next he was rolling in the dirt, shouting curses at the top of his lungs. The fall had busted up his right shoulder pretty badly. He gritted his teeth at the pain, knowing it was dislocated. His rifle lay several feet away from him as he had lost it in the fall.

The shrill cries of the things chasing him grew louder. They were almost on him now. His left hand jerked his Glock from where it hung, holstered on his hip. He painfully readied the weapon. There was nothing else he could do. The things were too close for it to matter if he started running again. He had no choice but to face them and die like the soldier he was.

Davis got to his feet, pointing the Glock at the sound of the closest shrieks. He couldn't see his target, only the tree limbs moving in its wake as the thing came crashing through them. Opening fire, he put a trio of rounds into the jungle where he figured the thing coming after him had to be. A loud screech let him know his fire had at least made contact with something.

Something cold and slimy lashed out and downwards from the tree behind him. It slipped around his neck and tightened there, lifting him from the ground. His feet kicked in the air as he smashed his pistol into it, desperately trying to break the thing's hold on him.

Davis couldn't breathe. His eyes bulged as the thing twisted about his neck grew tighter. The last sound Corporal Davis ever heard was the sickening snap of his own neck breaking.

****

Colonel Jackson Brannon had been out for his evening run when the black Suburban had picked him up. He sat next to Admiral Messer in its rear section, dripping sweat and sipping at the bottle of water the admiral had given him.

A clearly armed operative with an ear piece sat up front with the driver. Brannon had no doubt he was far from the only protection with eyes on Admiral Messer, though the Suburban appeared to be the only vehicle in this section of the park. This wasn't the first time he had been snatched up from leave when something had come up, but Messer's personal presence indicated that whatever it was this time, it was *really* bad.

"You always were a night owl." Messer feigned a smile.

"Could argue you were the one who made me this way, sir." Brannon smiled back.

Messer grunted. "Guess you could."

"We both know this isn't a social call, sir." Brannon pushed them on towards getting down to business. "Whose mess am I going to be cleaning up this time?"

Messer frowned and handed him a tablet. On its screen were the details of the job he was being drafted for. Brannon whistled as he read over them. When he looked up into Messer's eyes again, it was his turn to frown.

"Jones was one of the best. Not many people out there who are better," Brannon said.

"You are, Colonel," Messer said simply. "That's why I am here."

Brannon shook his head. "As to me being better than Jones, that's a matter of opinion, Admiral. I get what you are saying though. From the looks of what went down though, it ain't gonna be easy to clean it up."

"It never is." Messer sighed. "Not with something on the scale of this one."

"You have a plan though, or you wouldn't be here."

"Full-scale assault," Messer admitted. "It's the only option left to us now."

"Hard to keep that sort of thing off the public's radar," Brannon cautioned.

"Let me worry about that, Colonel," Messer said coldly.

"You know straight up fights aren't my thing anymore, sir," Brannon pointed out. "I left that for the regulars a long time ago."

Messer nodded. "That you did, but I need you on this one, Brannon. I need someone who can think outside the box and adapt to whatever crap storm they get tossed into. That's why I am putting you in command of the ground portion of this operation. We're not dealing with just another terrorist group here. These people bring a whole new meaning to the word cult.

"DESRON 44 is already in the area of the island. You and your squad will be flying out to join them. You have twelve hours to get your men and gear ready. Once you arrive, I expect you to work with Surface Commander Wall and take the lead in the planning the ground assault. Everything she has in terms of troops and firepower will be at your disposal. I want that cult wiped from the face of the Earth before the weekend is over. Do I make myself clear?"

"Crystal." Brannon grinned. "So much for my vacation, eh?"

****

Specialist Vander rolled over. His eyes bugged as he stared into the face of a strikingly beautiful blonde woman. Her long hair was spread over the pillow beneath her head. He spent a moment studying her features before he reached two conclusions. The first was that, try as he might, he could not recall her name. The second was that this woman was hotter than any human being had a right to be.

Ever so gently, he edged the covers over her back just enough to confirm his suspicion. Yep. She was naked underneath them. That certainly explained why he felt so relaxed and sore at the same time. Part of him wanted to pat himself on the back for a job well done, but the rest of him hated that he couldn't remember a bloody second of the passion the two of them were sure to have shared. That was the price of getting so drunk you couldn't see straight. His only comfort was the hope that when she woke up, she would want to make another go of it before life dragged them away from the bed they shared.

With a start, he realized it was his bed. He had brought her home. Given how hot she looked, Vander supposed he would have to forgive himself that one. Getting this lucky was a rare thing for him. He eased over on to his back and lay staring at the poster that lined the walls of his bedroom. Images of his hero stared back at him. His hero wore a thick, blue parka and carried a gun that was eighteen inches long and stopped molecular motion on an atomic level. Beneath the dark sunglasses he wore, his hero seemed to be smiling at him.

Vander had always loved the cold. He had grown up in rural Alaska and had always been a part of his life. Snow and ice, they were among the greatest gifts God had given man to Vander. He missed them a lot. Ever since he had signed up with Colonel Brannon, he had seen far too little of them. Sometimes he wondered if he had chosen the wrong career path. Sure, his job took him around the globe, but it was almost always to somewhere so hot and sunny that he couldn't stand it. Just once, he thought, he would like a mission to take them somewhere that wasn't a bloody jungle or desert. He knew it was a forlorn hope, but he persisted in it anyway.

As if in response to his thoughts, he heard the music of "Cold as Ice" begin to blare from his cell phone. Vander reached over, picking it up from the nightstand beside the bed. A quick glance at its screen told him the incoming call was from Colonel Brannon. He answered it.

"Vander here," he said. His cell was encrypted to Hades and then some. The line was as secure as anything could by in an age where hackers waged war against their enemies as if they were soldiers on the battlefield.

Vander held the phone with his neck and chin as snatched up a pen and notebook to jot down his orders. "Yes, sir," he said at last as Colonel Brannon ended the call.

Turning around where he sat on the edge of the bed, he saw the blonde watching him.

"Work?" she asked in the voice of an angel. Again, Vander cursed himself for not being sober when he had brought her home with him. "You never told me what you do."

"And I won't be now either, love." Vander frowned. "I've got to run. Duty calls."

Her hand reached out to spread flat against the bare, pale skin of his naked chest. "Do you really have to go so quickly?"

Vander laughed, calculating exactly how much time he needed to get dressed, gather his personal gear, and report in. "No," he smiled. "Maybe I don't."

He let her pull him down as she slid on top of him.

****

Adam sat at his desk. The room was dark. The only light was what little seeped into it through the window from the stars in the sky outside. He flicked ashes from the end of his cigarette into an already overflowing ashtray filled with two packs worth of butts.

He couldn't sleep. That was a problem a lot of folks in his line of work dealt with. When they closed their eyes, the faces of those they had killed or caused to be killed came clearly into focus like ghosts that refused to let them have any peace.

It was different for Adam though. He was at peace with his job. The face he saw was his wife's. Cancer had taken her from six months ago, and he hadn't been the same since. It was as if she had taken a bit of his soul with her when they had laid her to rest in the ground.

Adam liked to tell himself that he had done everything he could for her. He had called in favors with the powers that be to get her the best treatment possible and taken on extra jobs outside of usual channels to pay their medical bills. Nothing had worked though. She had grown weaker with each passing day until it reached the point he couldn't take it anymore. Then, he had truly buried himself in his work. Putting a bullet into some zealot's head and watching the man's brain matter splatter outward in a shower of gray and red was preferable to watching her waste away.

In short, he had run and had left her alone at the end. Oh, he sent checks, cards, gifts, and even called every day, but it wasn't the same as being there by her side. Until she had gotten sick, Adam had thought of himself as one of the bravest men alive and with good cause. He wasn't afraid of dying. He had been tortured by the best that the Middle East had at their disposal and hadn't broken. He had stared down the barrel of enemy guns and seen his friends blown apart by IED's. Adam had seen children caught in crossfire, their little bodies twitching as heavy rounds cut them to shreds. He had seen people crazy enough to slit their own throats for glory in the eyes of Allah. But all that, all of it, was nothing compared to watching Julie die. Not an honorable death as he hoped for himself one day but rather a prolonged, terrible wasting away to nothingness.

When he had finally returned home for her funeral and stared down at what was left of her resting in her coffin, he barely recognized the woman he had spent half his life with. She was little more than skin and bones. The spark in her eyes that had drawn him to her at the start, gone, replaced by the empty hollowness of death.

Often, Adam had considered taking his own life so he could be with her in Heaven but he knew doing so was an unforgivable sin in the eyes of God. Even more than that though, he knew he simply couldn't do it. To do so would be to admit defeat and that was something that Adam Hall could never do. It just wasn't in him.

He was glad to hear his phone ring. No one ever called him anymore unless it was about a job. Getting up from the table, he answered and was happy to hear Colonel Brannon's voice.

"Yes, sir," he barked into the phone. "I'm on my way in right now!"

As he shut off his phone, he took one last look at the picture of Julie that had been straining his eyes to stare at in the dark and said, "Goodbye, honey. Hope to see you again soon."

****

Sergeant Malcom Root stood at the doorway to his daughter's room, watching her sleep. He had tucked her in for the second time tonight only moments earlier. She had a bad dream and had come bursting into his and Steph's room. Unlike him, Steph worked a normal nine-to-five job and needed some sleep herself. Malcom had been happy to take Mary back to bed. She was his world and nothing mattered more to him, not even Steph. His job was the one that really paid the bills, but it only took him away from home every month or two and usually he wasn't gone very long. Just long enough to blow up whatever needed blowing up and then back to his family he came.

Malcom wanted very much to retire from it but knew he wouldn't until they had enough money tucked in the bank to make sure Mary was provided for life if he could. He wanted her to have all things his drunk, deadbeat of a father had never given him. Malcom dreamed of the day he would watch her walk across some college's stage, degree in hand. She would never know the pain of not having Santa show up on Christmas or the Easter bunny getting lost in route to her house. She would never see her mother shoved to the kitchen floor with a busted jaw and pummeled by the man who was supposed to love her. No, Malcom had vowed from the second Mary was born that her life would be as wonderful and perfect as he could make it, no matter the cost. His job was the only threat to that now. Every time he went out to answer his country's call, it no longer filled him with pride but rather left his heart broken until he could see his little girl again.

Steph appeared behind him, putting a hand on his shoulder. He nearly teared as he took the phone she shoved at him and said, "It's for you. Colonel Brannon."

She knew as much as he did what a phone call from the colonel meant. He saw the sadness in her expression as he raised the phone and spoke into it. "Can't say I am happy to hear from you, sir. It's not a good time..." Malcom frowned. "Yes, sir, I know it never is."

Malcom listened to his orders before he switched the phone off and handed back to Steph.

The two of them stared at each other in silence for a moment.

Finally, Steph said, "How soon?"

"Right now," Malcom admitted. "I should be moving already."

"I'm sorry," she said, hugging him to her.

"Me too," Malcom grunted.

"You can wake her up if you need to," Steph told him, nodding her head at where Mary lay in her bed, clutching a stuffed, pink pony in her arms.

Malcom gently removed himself from Steph's arms and shook his head. "I just got her back to bed and you need rest. Best I just go." His voice cracked as he said the words.

Steph nodded, knowing from experience not to argue with him.

"Tell her Daddy loves her and I will call as soon as I can."

Malcom didn't have the strength to say anything else. He kissed Steph and rushed down the hall to start packing up his gear without allowing himself to look back. He knew if he did, he wouldn't be able to leave.

****

Colonel Jackson Brannon was already aboard the copter that would be flying them out to meet up with DESRON 44 when his men arrived. Each of them brought him a strange comfort as they boarded: Vander with his cool as ice shades, self-assured swagger, and steady grip on the M24 he carried, Malcom with his ever so slightly ticked off yet stoic expression as the giant of a man that he was took his seat, and even Adam with his look of pent-up rage just waiting to be released on whatever target was put in front of him. Brannon loved them all in his own way. They were his brothers and his boys at once.

Their squad was short a man. Hamel had punched out during their last round on the sharp end. He had been a good guy and an excellent soldier, but everyone's time came sooner or later. His replacement was Corporal Jim Zahn, a young man with a service record that Brannon had to admit even impressed him. He had recruited Zahn himself but sadly hadn't had the chance to really get to know him yet. Brannon liked to know all the men under his command on a personal level. It made knowing what to expect from them in the heat of battle much easier. There was no time for it now either. Brannon knew he was just going to have trust his instincts about Zahn and hope for the best. The kid had a lot to live up to trying to fill Hamel's shoes in the eyes of the rest of the squad. This operation would determine whether the kid stayed on or got the boot depending on how things went, assuming the kid survived.

"Evening, Colonel." Vander grinned at him as he took his seat.

Brannon nodded at him, not knowing what else to say. He never did with Vander. The kid was a comic book and SF junkie to the core, so they didn't share a lot of common interests outside of guns, women, and their work. Small talk was pointless at a time like this anyway. Brannon needed to brief the whole squad during their flight, so as soon as they were all strapped in, settled, and had their helmet radios tuned into the squad's private channel, he got down to business.

"I am sure you've all heard of Colonel Jones and his Jackal Boys. Heck, we're usually the ones competing with them for the better rep. Well, this time, it's them we're cleaning up for," Brannon said.

"Whoa," Malcom cut in. "Are you saying the Jackal Boys got toasted? Jones is one tough mother, Colonel. I find that hard to believe."

Brannon nodded. "The Jackal Boys were the initial response to the mess we're headed into. They failed to deal with it. That's why we're here."

Malcom leaned back in his seat as if someone had gut-punched him. Brannon could hear the sergeant muttering obscenities under his breath even though Malcom had tried to keep them too quiet to be heard over the comlink the squad shared.

"Don't mean nothing," Adam grunted. "Don't change anything either. No matter who was there ahead of us, we're the ones who are gonna see the job through now."

Vander gave a slight, sideways tip of his head as the two fingers and thumb of his right hand made the shape of a gun, jerking as if firing a single shot.

Brannon retook control of the informal briefing by saying, "Look, we all know the Jackal Boys were good. Nobody's perfect though. We've all got an appointment with the reaper someday."

Pausing, Brannon cleared his throat before continuing. "The island that we're headed for, after meeting up with DESRON 44, is the suspected base of operations for a very dangerous and very whacko cult. We're not talking your run-of-the-mill extremists here. These guys make the rag-heads in the Middle East look sane by comparison. Their sole purpose is to make sure the human race bites the farm. They moved in and took over this island last year. Since then, they've been using it for Lord knows what but whatever they're using it for, you can bet it means something bad for the folks back home or we wouldn't be here."

"Bio-weapons?" Vander asked.

"More likely nukes," Adam butted in. "It's almost always nukes with groups like this."

Brannon shrugged. "No one really knows. Could be either or both, or maybe even something we've never seen before. All I can tell you for sure is that the Jackal Boys went in with orders to kill anything that moved and none of them ever came out. The last thing the ship that carried them in heard from them was screams according to the mission report."

"Just how many cultists are we expecting, sir?" Adam ran the fingers of his right hand over the metal of the M-16A4 he held in his lap.

"Best guess?" Brannon shrugged again. "At the very least dozens, more likely hundreds."

"And they expected one team to be able to handle them all?" Malcom demanded.

"Cool it, Malcom," Vander cautioned the sergeant. "We've dealt with numbers like that before ourselves. It's not that far outside the normal for an op like this and you know it."

"These cultists are for the most part untrained thugs," Brannon assured Malcom. "Vander's right. It's not like they were throwing the Jackal Boys up against professional soldiers. Even if that had been the case, you know it's a part of the job."

"I've been trying to leave the job, sir," Malcom shot back at him. "Some colonel I owe a lot to keeps dragging me back into it."

Brannon flinched but otherwise kept his demeanor professional. "If I thought I could have pulled this off without you, Malcom, you know I would have tried."

Malcom's expression spoke volumes about just how much he appeared to believe what Brannon had said.

"This will be your last op, Sergeant," Brannon told him, meaning it. "No matter how many strings I have to pull, I'll see to it. I do need you on this one though."

"This DESRON we're meeting up with," Vander changed the subject, "I take it that means we'll have support?"

Brannon frowned. "More support than we want. There are several squads of marines that will be joining us for the show on the island."

"Oh, isn't that bleeding wonderful," Vander whined.

"You've got to be kidding, right?" Adam hissed. "They expect us to babysit too?"

"I said marines," Brannon reminded the others. "You will treat them and their CO with respect, understood?"

No one answered. Brannon understood the feeling of superiority that came from being part of a squad like their own, but he couldn't allow it to get in the way of what they needed to accomplish on the island. His Reapers were just going to have to accept that even they had to work with help sometimes. They had no problem with air support or ships laying down fire from sea, but tell them they had to share the ground with "common grunts" even if those grunts were freaking marines and they got uppity about it.

"Maybe I didn't make myself clear," Brannon snarled at the three of them. "We're going to show them the respect they deserve as marines."

Vander nodded and flashed him a grin. "Sure thing, boss, you got it."

"Yes, sir," Malcom echoed the sniper's agreement.

Adam's features were still twisted in an expression of disgust and contempt. "You know how I feel about being tossed onto the sharp end with folks I don't know."

"I didn't say I liked it either, Adam," Brannon pointed out.

Finally, Adam nodded, "Orders are orders I suppose, sir."

"Good." Brannon smiled. "Glad we got that dealt with here and now."

Brannon had read Adam's last psych-evaluation again on the road to the base their copter had just launched from. He hadn't liked what he had read it in either but Adam, like the rest of the Reapers, was worth the risks that came with him when you were basically walking into Hell. Even so, Brannon made a mental note to keep an eye on Adam. If the man lost it in the field, he would put him down himself if need be.

The newbie, Zahn, had kept quiet through it all, perhaps not feeling he had a right to speak up yet. For now, Brannon was okay with that. The kid would either fit in or not, only time and combat would tell.

The flight was a short one. The copter flew over the waves, under cover of night, and approached the ships that made up DESRON 44. As the DESRON came into view, Brannon was surprised to see how small it was. DESRON 44 was composed of only two destroyers and three frigates. He had no idea it would be such an understrength squadron, but it made sense. With the powers that be back home wanting to keep the assault on the island as quiet as possible, keeping the number of ships involved to a bare minimum was only logical.

"If that's a DESRON then I'm a bloody metahuman." Vander laughed.

"Don't," Adam warned the sniper. "You start talking that geek crap, and I'll toss you out of this bird to shut you up if I have to. You know I can't stomach it."

"Just because you have no appreciation or understanding of pop culture, good sir," Vander leaned forward in his seat, "doesn't mean the rest of us don't."

"Enough." Brannon stared at the two of them.

Vander held up his hands, showing Brannon his palms, in a mock expression of surrender. "He started it, sir, not me."

Adam appeared on the verge of unstrapping himself so he could have a go at Vander right there in the rear of the copter.

"Specialist Hall, restrain yourself," Brannon ordered Adam.

Adam slumped back into his seat. "Just keep him quiet about all that kid junk and we're cool, sir."

"You heard the man, Vander," Brannon said. "Let's all try to stay focused on whatever might be waiting for us on that island."

The copter touched down on the helipad of the USS *Nightstalker.* As the Reapers disembarked with Brannon in the lead, Surface Commander Wall, a man who was clearly her XO, and two armed marines stood in the rain that was pouring from the night sky waiting on them.

"Permission to come aboard, ma'am?" Brannon asked, giving Wall a salute.

"Permission granted, Colonel." Wall smiled at him. "It's about time you and your boys got here."

"Thank you, ma'am," Brannon answered formally.

****

Captain Wall and her XO, Franklin, stood gathered around the planning table with Brannon and Malcom. Brannon had sent Vander, Adam, and Zahn on to meet up with the marines that would be their support on the op.

A satellite imagery map of the island was rolled out on the table's top and Brannon proceeded to tell Captain Wall what he thought was the best approach to taking the island with as few causalities as possible. Captain Wall was far from happy with his plan.

"So, let me get this straight, Colonel," Wall said, tapping her fingers on the map at the spot where the island's southern-most beach was located. "You want to use my marines as bait?"

"Not bait, ma'am. I want to use them as a distraction. It's not quite the same thing," Brannon answered.

Captain Wall glared at him. "I understand that, Colonel, but I still have an issue with you throwing my men into the grinder if there's a better approach that we can use."

"There isn't," Malcom chimed in. Brannon shot him a look that told him to keep his mouth shut. Malcom either didn't notice or care because he went on, "Captain, your men are used to stand-up fights. They can handle it. And frankly, if the cultists are busy raining fire down on them, it leaves us free to move and get the job here done."

Sarah Wall was young to be in command of a DESRON. Heck, she was young to be a captain from Brannon's experience, but she sure appeared to know her stuff. Her actual rank title was COMDESRON 44, but that was a mouthful, so everyone just kept it to captain as she was also the captain of the *Nightstalker*. It was admittedly a slightly strange thing to do, but it seemed to work for Wall and her crew, so Brannon had just accepted and ran with it. If the lady wanted to be called captain, it wasn't his place to say otherwise.

She was a dang attractive woman too, and no matter how professional and competent she came across, there was no hiding that fact. The male brain was wired to notice things like that and it was only human to do so.

Captain Sarah Wall stood roughly five foot six and her body was hard and toned beneath her uniform. She wasn't the sort of officer who let herself go because she sat behind a desk pushing papers and making the hard calls when the crap hit the fan.

Her hair was "bob cut" and followed the curves of her face. Its color was dark blonde and made sharper the color of her fierce, intelligent, blue eyes. Her figure, though boyish in terms of her upper body, was all female from the waist down. More than once, Brannon had to put effort into forcing himself not to check out the butt covered by the tight pants of her uniform. He was sure that Wall was used to such things being trapped at sea with a ship full of men away from their wives and girlfriends, but he was also equally sure she would put him on the deck with a broken jaw if she caught him.

"Colonel?" she asked, ripping Brannon out of his inappropriate thoughts. "Do you agree with your man's assessment?"

"I do, ma'am," Brannon answered, a bit too quickly. He caught himself and added, "I think it's the only approach that's going to work. We're dealing with an enemy force of unknown size. Better to get them to come to us and put them on the defensive so we can really get a feel for what they have rather than go in completely blind. Any of your men that we lose, well, the info and time their lives buy us might make the difference on how all this plays out."

Wall nodded. "My orders said that you were to have complete command over the assault on the island and how it was to be carried out. I want it on record though that I protested this approach."

"Understood," Brannon said, matching the coldness of her tone. She and Vander would certainly get along, he thought. It was a good thing he had sent Vander on to meet with the marines or he might have a whole other problem to deal with as if there wasn't enough on his plate already.

"I want your ships ready to lay down some a massive rain of carnage if we need it," Brannon said. "I don't think it will come to that but one never knows."

"We'll be ready should the need arise," Captain Wall assured him.

"Good." Brannon smiled. "At dawn then…"

"At dawn." Captain Wall nodded.

****

Lieutenant Dustin Sharps wasn't at all happy about a squad of elite special ops having command over him and his men. Wasn't much he could do about it though as the boats carrying his platoon splashed towards the island's beach. This wasn't his first combat landing on a beach, but they never got any easier. It was like playing Russian roulette. You never knew who was going to catch it from the enemy until a round blew a hole in you and you were either dead or lying in the sand.

Each of the three small boats carried ten marines, all under his command. They hit the beach in unison, his men spreading out and taking up defensive positions. As yet, they hadn't seen any indication that the bad guys even knew they were coming. Not that Sharps was going to complain about that. He knew at any moment the beach could turn into a hot zone of flying bullets and the screams of dying men.

Sharps kept his eyes on the trees above the beach as his men secured their position. When still no resistance came, they moved forward. His fingers tapped the comlink on his helmet as he reported in.

"Alpha platoon has landed. No resistance. We're moving inland," he said before following his men towards the trees.

The lack of resistance was both surprising and disturbing. Sharps had been briefed to expect the cultists on the island to come at them with everything they had.

"Where the hell are they, LT?" Corporal Perron whispered as Sharps caught up to him.

Sharps didn't have an answer as the platoon continued to move inland. The trees and foliage opened onto a road. Sharps held up a fist signaling the rest of the platoon to halt. There was something sitting in the middle of the road. It appeared to be a small convoy of jeeps. There were men all around the vehicles, but they were all down. Dried blood stained the sides and open interiors of the jeeps as well as the ground around them. Had the special ops guys hit them already? Rationally, Sharps knew that was impossible. Their sniper had been dropped on the other side of the island an hour ago, but there was no way he could have made it here that fast even if he had run straight out without stopping. And the rest of the sniper's unit wasn't supposed to be anywhere near here either. They were supposed to be heading from the cultist's compound where it lay at the island's center.

The men around the jeeps were dead though. Of that, there was no question. Sharps motioned for his men to advance on the mess in the road and followed them out of the trees. The closer he got to the carnage on the road, the more disturbing it became. The men around the jeeps hadn't been shot. They had been torn apart. Some of them were missing arms or legs. Others had their heads ripped completely from their shoulders … and there was no sign of those missing heads.

One cultist lay sprawled over the hood of a jeep, his open, vacant eyes staring up into the rising sun. The entire middle portion of his body had been dug into. Long, bloated strands of his intestines snaked from the mess that was his stomach to rest in the dirt below where his feet dangled. His mouth was fixed into a permanent, rigid scream.

Another cultist was face down next to a jeep with a piece of his broken spine sticking up from his mangled back as if something had yanked it partially out of him and was driven away before it finished the grizzly work of removing it completely.

Shell casings and spent round were everywhere. These men had put up a fight and a dang good one from the look of things, but there was no one else on the road except for them. Whoever or whatever had done this either hadn't taken any losses or had carried away their own dead as they withdrew with the battle was over.

"LT!" Perron shouted. "You better come and look at this, sir!"

Sharps rushed to where Perron knelt beside the corpse of one of the dead cultists.

"These men…" Perron stammered as if in shock, "they've been eaten on, sir."

"What?" Sharps rasped.

"Look, sir," Perron pointed at the corpse, "I'm a park ranger back home. These wounds here and here, they're bite-marks, sir. Never seen ones like them, but I swear that's what they are. You can see the tears where the teeth took out chunks of this guy."

"Holy frag," Sharps breathed, having known Perron long enough to trust his call.

"What in the devil are we up against here, LT?" Perron asked.

"Maybe these guys are cannibals and they turned on each other before we got here," Sharps said and knew it was as lame of an explanation as it sounded even as he said the words.

"Doesn't add up and you know it, LT." Perron shook his head. "These bite marks aren't human."

Perron rolled the corpse over. "Not a bullet hole anywhere in this guy, LT. None of the others that I've seen either. Whatever killed these guys did it fast and 'tooth and nail.'"

Suddenly, an eerie feeling hit Sharps. He felt like they were being watched.

He walked over to one of the jeeps. Its driver's seat was soaked in blood. He reached out and touched it. The blood was dried and cold. "Whatever happened here, it happened a good while before we even hit the beach."

"I know," Perron nodded. "Creeps me out, LT."

"Me too." Sharps gave Perron a nod. "Good work, Perron."

"What the Hell do we do now, LT?"

Sharps thought the situation over before he made his call. "We're going to hold up here and call this in. Pass along the word to stay sharp," he ordered Perron. "Whatever did this could still be out there in those trees somewhere."

"Yes, sir," Perron snapped as he got to his feet and scurried off to where the rest of the platoon was positioning themselves to form a secure perimeter around the jeeps.

Sharps said a silent prayer that they were going to be able to get the Hell off the island before they found out what killed the cultists. From the looks of things, meeting up with whatever was responsible for this mess would be an experience he didn't want to have.

****

Colonel Jackson Brannon, though several miles distant from Lieutenant Sharps and his men, was feeling much the same. In his career, he had seen a lot of things, but never anything like this island. As he stood in the command center of the base at the heart of the island, Brannon knew beyond a shadow of a doubt that all the cultists were dead. On their trip to the command center and inside it, he, Adam, and Malcom had found only corpses—ripped apart and pecked at corpses. The bodies and pieces of bodies that they had come across all shared similar wounds that told him that whatever had killed the cultists had also feasted on them. Some of the cultists were nearly picked down to their bones. Their flesh had been sheared and sliced away. However, there were also other wounds that that actually did more closely resemble teeth marks. Often around those were circles where it looked as if the victim's blood had been sucked upwards to the surface beneath their skin. No human being using any weapon Brannon could think of could have killed the cultists in such a fashion. No, there was something else at work here, something else on this island with them. Whatever it, or more likely they, were, they had done the hard part of the Reapers' work for them. Brannon and his men hadn't needed to fire a single shot during their entire time on the island.

The command center's main ops room looked as if a tornado of spears and teeth had swept through it. The bodies of dead cultists lay amid a sea of shattered computer screen and damaged surveillance stations. The whole base was running on emergency power and the eerie, red lighting only served to freak Brannon out more. It also made the pools of fresher blood covering the floor more difficult to see. One had to be careful not to slip moving around on the entrails-smeared floor.

Adam was barely holding it together. The man had been dangerously on the edge of breaking before they had taken this op, and its strangeness was pushing him over the edge. If he had been bloodthirsty before, he was ready to explode in a fury of rage on anything that gave him the chance to now.

Malcom wasn't holding up much better. He looked scared out of his mind and with good reason. Brannon had kept a mental count of the cultist bodies they found both on their way in and inside the cultists' command center. There were over sixty of them. Anything that could make such short work of so many armed men, trained or not, was something to worry over. Odds were whatever killed the cultists was still here, hiding, maybe waiting for the right moment to hit them too. They needed to gather what intel they could and get out before it had the chance.

Every member of the Reapers had at least two specialties. Unfortunately, Vander was their tech/computer guy and he wasn't with them. He should have met up with and checked in as they reached the command center, but they hadn't heard a peep out of him yet. Vander was keeping to radio silence as he usually did. Brannon wasn't worried enough about his lack of contact yet to break it. The marines on the beach were using a frequency that his squad could overhear and were under no such constraints as his squad was the stealth part of the op. He had heard their report of similar findings in terms of dead cultists when they had called it in to Captain Wall on the *Nightstalker,* confirming his suspicion that all the cultists had been eliminated by an unknown force.

Vander or not, they needed to learn what they could from the cultists' computers. Brannon took a flash-drive from one of the pouches on his belt and plugged it into what appeared to the main computer in the room. He grumbled as he fought to download data from it to the drive. Thankfully, the cultists appeared to have been smug enough not to encrypt anything. He imagined they never thought anyone would ever make it this deep into their base.

When the transfer was complete, Brannon pulled the drive and carefully tucked it away. Malcom was moving about the room, better inspecting the damage that had been done to its equipment while Adam stood, nervously, by the room's entrance, his M-16a4 at the ready.

"We've got what we came for," Brannon told them. "Let's go find Vander and get back to the ship ASAP."

****

Lieutenant Sharps opened fire as all Hell broke loose around him. No one had seen the attack coming. He and his men had left the road and were headed back to the beach when the things showed themselves. They seemed to come from everywhere at once. Some bounded through the trees, hitting the flanks of his men's formation. Others simply dropped out of the trees onto them. In less than twenty seconds, half his men were dead and the rest were fighting for their lives.

The *things* were some sort of messed-up squids. They moved by using their primary two tentacles like legs or insanely strong arms. Their movements reminded Sharps of the long arms of apes as they bounded across a jungle clearing. They came at Sharps and his men fast and hard, rolling into them in the blink of an eye.

The first of Sharps' marines to die had taken one of those larger tentacles directly through his chest. It stabbed into and through him like a spear, plunging out his back in a spray of blood. The marine hadn't even had time to scream. And he was only the first to die.

In a matter of seconds, half of Sharps' platoon was either dead or on the ground, bleeding out. His men were trying to fight back though. M-16 fire chattered and barked, echoing among the trees along with the screams of his men who did have time to cry out as they died.

Lieutenant Sharps took aim at one of the squid monsters as it bolted passed him towards an utterly stunned Corporal Perron. He squeezed the trigger of his M-16, letting loose a three-round burst. It caught the squid on its side. The rounds shredded its flesh and sent the creature tumbling to land in the dirt. A thick blackish blood leaked from its wounds as the squid-thing shrieked, thrashing where it lay. Sharps ran over to it, firing a second burst into the creature at point blank range to make sure it stayed down.

It was Perron's turn to save him. Sharps didn't see the squid that dropped from the tree behind him. A burst from the corporal's rifle met the squid creature as it fell towards Sharps. The creature's black blood splattered over Sharps, but Perron's burst had kept the squid from landing on top of him. Sharps whirled to fire into the creature as it tried to lash out at him with its primary tentacles. His burst struck the squid dead on in its central mass, reducing its main body to little more than exploding pulp.

"Grenade!" Sharps heard Perron shout as the corporal lobbed one into a trio of the squid-things that were racing towards them. The grenade detonated in the path of the creatures, spraying them with shrapnel. It tore their bodies apart in a bright flash of orange.

Lieutenant Sharps knew his men were fighting a losing battle. There were too many of the squid creatures to fight in the jungle like this. The creatures had the advantage here. The things were using the cover of the trees to shield themselves from his men's fire, and worse, were using the trees as means to move even faster than the creatures did on the ground. They were swinging in on their limbs and flinging themselves into his men too quickly to be stopped. His men were being overrun despite the firepower they brought to bear on the monsters. He wanted to give the order to fall back but there was nowhere to fallback to. Both the road where the monsters had taken out the convoy of cultists and the beach were too far away. They would never make if they tried for either. All he and his men could do was hold their ground and hope the squids stopped coming.

Turning to Corporal Perron, Sharps felt his mouth drop open in shock. Perron dangled in the air. Several of the squids in a tree above the corporal had grabbed a hold of the man and had Perron in the grasp of their tentacles. Perron's rifle lay on the ground below him as he struggled against the squids.

Sharps could hear the corporal's muffled grunts of pain. They would have been screams, but one of the tentacles was wrapped about his face, covering his mouth. Then Perron was dead. Two of the squids tugged on him in opposite directions with such force the corporal's body gave and tore apart down the middle.

In the wake of that moment of horror, Sharps realized he was alone. All of his men were dead. He was the last human standing. Squids moved about, their beak-like mouths tearing into the corpses of his men, slicing away chunks of flesh that they gobbled up with astonishing speed.

Two squids came lunging at him. Sharps managed to get off a burst that ripped through one of the two squids' central mass and sent it careening sideways to tumble onto the jungle floor. The other smashed into him like a linebacker. The force of the impact knocked Sharps from his feet with the sound of his ribs cracking and snapping inside his chest. He tasted his own blood rising up into his mouth. The squid had already hoisted itself back up to stand on its two primary tentacles, towering over him. Its lesser tentacles writhed about angrily in the air beneath it.

Sharps jerked the barrel of his rifle into position to fire up into the creature's underside but never got the chance. Two of its lesser tentacles snatched his rifle by its barrel and yanked it from his grasp. The squid flung the rifle away into the jungle around them. Sharps reached for a grenade on his belt. He didn't try to free it but rather pulled its pin. When the squid dove onto him, the two of them vanished in a blast of fire and exploding shrapnel.

****

It hadn't taken Vander long to have an encounter with the squid-like monsters on the island once he had been dropped off on it. He had spotted them the first time from nearly a mile away through his scope. Vander found their odd appearance and bizarre movements almost comical until he had seen the things in action.

Vander had witnessed the massacre of Lieutenant Sharps and his men. In the jungle of the island, like any other, Vander was a ghost. No one ever saw him unless he wanted them to. So far, that had seemed to hold true for the squids as well. He had kept his distance from them and hadn't engaged the creatures. After seeing what they had done to Sharps' troops, he was glad he had. He was

34

a sniper and never intended to be up close to any target when he sent it to Hell, but that didn't mean he was always lucky enough to not be noticed when he opened up.

Now Vander was on the run. He, too, had stumbled upon the mostly devoured bodies of several cultists and knew from what happened to Sharps' men that the cultists were likely all dead. Still, he didn't break radio silence just in case he was wrong. He didn't want to tip off any cultists that might have survived whatever the squid-things were that the Reapers were on the island.

Vander couldn't remember the last time before today that he had truly been afraid for his life. Whatever the squid things were though, they spooked him. Everything about them made him think of the word abomination. Creatures like them shouldn't exist in the real world. They were the stuff of late-night B -movies on the horror channel.

All he wanted to do was make it to the beach, find his boat, and get back onboard the *Nightstalker*. He hadn't seen any of the squid monsters in the water, but from the look of them, they would be even more deadly there than on the land. That worried him. The small boat he came ashore in was an open one. He didn't have a lot of faith that it would do the job of getting him back to the *Nightstalker* safely.

Vander skidded to a halt in the jungle, considering the option of making for the enemy command center where he was supposed to have met up with the rest of the Reapers. Heading there would mean more time in the trees, so he questioned if it was worth the risk to try for the command center. There was no guarantee that Brannon and the team were still there. Given the amount of time that had passed since they had all landed on the island, they, too, might already be headed back for the ship.

He paced his breathing, trying to calm himself. In addition to the M24 he carried, Vander also had an UZI that swung by side from a shoulder strap and a custom-made Glock holstered on his hip. He longed for his Barrett M84, but he left the rifle on the ship. Usually, he preferred the simplicity of the M24 to the M84, but today, he missed its firepower and rate of fire compared to that of the M24.

His instincts and what he saw of the squids told him they hunted their prey by sound. It was a lot easier to move about unseen than unheard. He didn't trust even his level of skill at stealth to avoid the monsters in this jungle. He knew they liked to use the trees to move about more than to bounce around on their primary tentacles on the ground. Using their tentacles to swing from limb to limb was likely easier for them given the strength of their limbs and the density of the jungle's trees. And the monsters were crazy fast. Vander had been a runner all his life, but he knew the squids could overtake him with little effort if they detected him.

Vander leaped into motion again, sprinting onward towards the beach. He remained unconvinced that taking the boat back to the ship was his best option. He hoped instead that he could find somewhere on the beach to hide. He was good at hiding. If he could just hunker down somewhere out of sight, he could wait until either help stumbled onto him or he feel better about breaking radio silence to call in an extraction.

His legs pumped beneath him as he broke from the trees, and the soles of his heavy boots started kicking up the sand of the beach as he ran onward. He spotted a cluster of rocks that had an opening in them in the shape of a wedge. He could hide there and be able to have a view of the tree line as long as there was nothing waiting for him already in the rocks.

Vander slowed his pace, slinging his M24 onto his back by its straps and readied his UZI. He approached the rocks quickly but with great caution, keeping his eyes trained on the darkness of the small hole within them. Vander gave an exhausted sigh of relief as he saw the space in the cluster of rocks was unoccupied and eased into it. He shifted himself around, trading his UZI for his M24 once again. He took aim at the trees through the M24's scope and settled in, hoping he wouldn't have to wait long for help to arrive. Vander figured if no one showed in an hour or so, he would cave in and break radio silence. By then, surely, it would be safe to do.

****

Captain Wall paced the bridge of the *Nightstalker*. She had known Lieutenant Sharps ever since she had taken command of the ship. He was a good man and a good officer. Wall had listened to the screams of Sharps and his men as they died on the island. So many dead and for what? The cultists had been wiped out before Sharps and his men even arrived. Part of her wanted to blame to Colonel Jackson for his plan that had put her marines into danger. She knew that was irrational and a purely emotional response to the disaster that the raid on the island had become. Sarah Wall liked to think she was above such things these days, but she knew she was only human.

The member of the Reapers, Zahn, which had remained on the ship, approached her.

"Ma'am, I am sorry about your men, but Colonel Jackson and the Reapers are still on that island," he reminded her. "We have to do something before we lose them too."

Franklin, her XO, cleared his throat. "Captain Wall is aware of the situation, son."

"He's right, Franklin," Wall said. "We need to do something."

"But ma'am, we don't even know what's really happening over there. What can we do?" Franklin protested. "Surely you don't believe that our marines were really just wiped out by squids."

"At this point, I don't know what to believe, but none the less, we must act." Wall shook her head.

"The attack on your marines happened so fast, it's impossible to know for sure what hit them, on that I agree." Zahn's voice was strained. "I'm not ready to believe in monsters either just yet, but whatever took them out doesn't matter. The Reapers are in danger, ma'am, and it's your duty to get them out if they can."

"Watch it, son!" Franklin bellowed.

"Franklin!" Wall snapped at her XO. "We still have the helicopter that delivered your squad on hand," she told Zahn. "Franklin, I want that bird in the air and bound for the island in the next five. Tell the pilot to make a sweep of the island and pick up any of our men or the Reapers that it can. No arguments!"

"Yes, ma'am." Franklin nodded and raced off to carry out the order.

"Thank you, Captain Wall," Zahn said sincerely, the relief he felt clear in his voice.

****

Colonel Jackson Brannon was the first of the three Reapers to emerge from the woods onto the beach. Malcom followed closely after him. Adam brought up the rear, watching the trees. They had no clue what had wiped out the cultists and Brannon didn't want to find out. All he wanted was to get off the island as quickly as they could. He hoped the flash-drive, tucked inside one of the pouches on his belt, would provide all the answers they needed. They all had heard the cries of Lieutenant Sharps and his men as *something* had engaged the marines and taken them out. The words "squids" and "monsters" had been shouted a few times amid the roar of gunfire and screams before the lieutenant's platoon had fallen silent. Even after seeing the level of destruction inside the cultists' command center and the picked at bodies of the dead, he wasn't quite ready to believe in monsters just yet. None the less, he was worried. Whatever they were dealing with here, it was certainly something new that they had never encountered before. And in situations like this one, new was never a good thing.

There was still no sign of Vander, and that worried him even more. Vander had more kills and combat missions than the rest of them added together, despite his age. It made Brannon glad they had left the squad's new member, Corporal Zahn, on the *Nightstalker* to act as the Reapers' liaison there. Zahn had protested that call furiously, and Brannon knew he was insulted by it. Brannon had planned to take the kid along with them right up until the last minute, but something inside of him had warned him otherwise then. Zahn would get over the insult. Right now, Brannon needed the men he had spilled blood with and he knew could handle whatever came at them. The Reapers functioned like a well-oiled machine, and the kid would have only screwed that up, regardless of how good he might be.

"Colonel!" Adam shouted suddenly. Both Brannon and Malcom spun around to see the woods above the beach swarming with bizarre creatures that appeared to be land-based squids. The things came swinging through the trees, hurling themselves from limb to limb with their tentacles. Brannon had been in the process of lighting up a cigarette. It dangled from his lips for a moment before it fell to the ground at his feet.

Adam was backpedaling towards where the two of them stood, staring in disbelief at what they saw. The squid-things hurled themselves by the dozens onto the sand, picking themselves up with their primary two tentacles acting like legs, to come bounding forward.

Not waiting for an order to do so, Adam started blasting away at the squids. His M-16 bucked in his hands as he fired a continued barrage of three-round bursts in the monsters. Malcom's grenade launcher thunked as he popped one into the center of the advancing mass of squids. The ensuing explosion ripped a good number of the squids to piece and rained black blood over the beach.

Brannon picked target after target. Each time, he would choose a squid, blow it to Hell with a well-aimed burst to its central mass, and then move onto the next one. The barrel of his M-16 swept back and forth as he kept his targets to the closest of the squids instead of the ones still coming from the trees. There were just too many of the things. Despite his effort, two of them made it through. They were closing on him as his rifle clicked empty. Brannon jerked the spent magazine from the weapon but had no time to shove another home. The chattering fire of an UZI rang out as Vander appeared, seemingly out of nowhere, at his side.

Vander's stream of fire reduced the two squids to piles of mangled flesh.

"Miss me?" The sniper quipped over the sounds of the battle as Brannon slammed a fresh magazine into his M-16, locking it into place.

The Reapers were together again. All four members of the squad were making a fighting retreat towards the water and the assault boat that rocked on the waves there. The number of squid creatures emerging from the trees was growing.

"We're not gonna make it!" Malcom shouted even as he flung his M-16 aside, having emptied the weapon's last magazine, and drew the sawed-off, pump-action shotgun from the holster on his right leg. He worked a shell in its chamber as one of the faster squids reached him. Its tentacles whipped outwards, swiping at his face. Malcom narrowly avoided the attack, jerking his head back and away at the last second. The squid sprang as Malcom tried to recover his balance. A three-round burst ripped into the squid as Adam saved his life. It flung the squid sideways as the bullets left gaping holes in its body. Black blood splashed over Malcom. He tried desperately to wipe it from his skin as he continued retreating but only succeeded in smearing it more widely across his cheeks and face. Some of it got into his mouth. He spat it out, but the taste left him gagging.

The sound of an approaching helicopter drew Brannon's attention skyward. The bird they had flown to meet the

Nightstalker aboard came sweeping in over the beach. Its side gunner hosed the squids on the beach fifty-caliber fire. The squids were either too driven or too stupid to even attempt to dodge it. The high-powered rounds shredded the monsters, soaking the sand with the black oil that was their blood.

The copter touched down between the Reapers and the tree line. The gunner kept up his rate of fire trying to hold back the squids that continued to pour from the trees. Brannon and the other Reapers wasted no time in racing for the copter. They were all aboard it in less than a minute.

"Get us out of here!" Brannon screamed at the bird's pilot.

"Already on it!" the pilot shouted, flipping switches above him before he got the copter into motion again. The helicopter rose into the blue sky, leaving the island and the squids behind it.

Brannon watched the squid creatures swarming over the beach as the helicopter's pilot got his bearings and headed towards the *Nightstalker*. Where had they come from? Just how many of the things were there? And most importantly, were the creatures contained to the island and the waters surrounding it?

****

Brannon was glad to be onboard the *Nightstalker* again. In his years in the service, he had been through a lot of stuff, but he had never encountered actual, literal monsters before. The experience was unsettling to say the least. He was more worried about Adam now than ever. The man had been on the edge of a breakdown before. Who knew what effect living through something like they just had would have on him?

Malcom, on the other hand, was holding up even better than he was himself despite that Captain Wall had ordered him quarantined due to his direct exposure to the blood of the things they had encountered. The man had been covered in the black oily substance that was the squids' blood when he came aboard the ship and openly admitted it had gotten into his mouth. If Malcom was concerned about something happening to him from the exposure, he didn't show it. He was taking the whole mess in stride and seemed to just be happy to be off the sharp end.

As to Vander, well, he was Vander. It was all just another op to him, monsters or not.

Captain Wall had called a meeting within an hour of Brannon's return and he was headed to it now. The cultists were gone, yes, but the question had become what to do about the squid creatures. Brannon had his own thoughts on that, but it was really Captain Wall's call at this point.

As he walked towards the meeting room, Wall's XO Franklin emerged from the doorway of his office to join him.

"Colonel," Franklin greeted him.

Brannon gave Franklin a nod as the two of them walked on towards the meeting room side by side.

"So I guess there really are monsters in this world after all," Franklin commented.

Brannon grunted.

Captain Wall was waiting for them as they entered and took their seats at the conference table.

Brannon dove straight into business. "Have your techs been able to take a look at the drive I brought aboard?"

"Yes." Wall's hands rested, fingers intertwined on the table top in front of her. "The squid creatures you and your men encountered are the direct result of the bio-engineering project the cultists were running on the island. It appears their attempts to awaken, and I quote, 'the ancient god,' that was supposed to be in a dormant state below the waters of this region failed. As thus, they turned to trying to create that god themselves. These squids that can move about on land are their creation. According to the files you brought, these things multiply at a rate that could threaten humanity's control of the oceans and perhaps, one day, even lead to a land war with them as well."

Brannon and Franklin were silent as Wall continued.

"These creatures are driven by only two directives—devour whatever living things cross their path and breed. The drive doesn't contain information on how they escaped the cultists' control, but it put their number in the high thousands."

"Thousands?" Franklin repeated the word in disbelief.

"Thousands," Wall confirmed. "The cultists apparently believed that number was possibly even on the low side at the end."

"Then, Captain," Brannon cut in, "we have to stop these things here and now. If they were to truly spread beyond this region, the cultists are correct in the level of threat they could be to the human race as a whole."

Captain Wall nodded. "At this time, the bulk of the squids appear on the island but not all of them. I have ordered the *Nightstalker* to a high-alert status and set up a watch for any squids that might make a move against her."

"Do you really believe those things could be a threat to this ship, ma'am?" Franklin asked.

"The cultists wanted to bring about the downfall of the human race. The loss of Lieutenant Sharps and his men is proof of just how dangerous the squids are. There is no reason to think they aren't just as deadly in the water as they are on land."

Brannon knew Franklin couldn't argue with that assumption, though the XO really looked like he wanted to. It was as if the man couldn't truly accept what was happening here.

"Have you reported the situation here to the higher ups back home, Captain?" Brannon asked.

"Funny you should ask that, Colonel." Wall's lower lip twitched. "For some reason my techs haven't figured out yet, we've lost all long-range communications."

"How is that possible?" Brannon frowned.

"As I said, we don't know. There's some sort of electro-magnetic interference in the area. So far, it's only affecting our comm. systems, but the techs tell me it's getting stronger every hour."

"So we're alone out here?" Brannon asked. "That's all the more reason for us to act now while we still can. If those squids—"

"Let me assure you that I agree, Colonel," Captain Wall interrupted him. "DESRON 44 has two destroyers within its numbers. I plan to hit the island with everything they have short of nukes. We'll slag the island."

"That's a good plan," Brannon agreed, impressed by Wall's planned response to the situation. "And then?"

"Then we get the Hell of here and let someone else deal with the rest." Captain Wall smiled.

****

Sonar Tech Andy Carter loved his job most days. He got to travel the world while helping make it a safer place. Today though was one of the dark days that came with the job. He had known most of the marines the *Nightstalker* and DESRON 44 had sent ashore as part of the op to clear the island. Andy had said a prayer for their families as he sat at his station on the *Nightstalker's* bridge. Captain Wall had ordered the ship to a high-alert status, so he was running constant sweeps of the waters around her, or rather his, computer was. The sweeps had picked up some smaller anomalies that he supposed were the squid creatures that he had been told about. The number of anomalies he was picking up was far too few and too distant to be of any concern as yet. Andy kept a watch on them. It was hard to believe he was on the lookout for mutant, killer squids. Yeah, sure, they weren't really mutants. They had been created by men, crazy men intent on ending the world.

Andy snapped to attention at his station as Captain Wall came onto the bridge. The XO and Colonel Brannon followed her. He listened as the XO set up a coordinated strike on the island by the *Nightstalker* and her sister ship, the *Ares.* The sheer amount of firepower that was about to rain down on the island was staggering. Andy had never been a part of anything remotely like it before.

As Franklin was finishing up the coordinating of the strike, he noticed Captain Wall coming towards him.

"Carter, I need to know how many squids make it off the island during the strike," she told him. "We need to wipe those things out as entirely as we can. If you detect any large groups of the things moving into the water, I want you to pass that information directly to fire control."

"Yes, ma'am," Andy answered. The same interference that was affecting the comm. systems was beginning to creep into messing with the ship's sonar too, but not beyond anything he hadn't been able to deal with.

He watched as Captain Wall returned to her place on the bridge and got ready to give the order for the strike on the island to commence.

"We ready?" she asked Franklin.

The XO nodded.

"Take target with guns," Captain Wall ordered. "I don't want anything over there to survive this. Understood?"

Night was beginning to fall over the island. The *Nightstalker* and the *Ares* lit it up with streaks of orange, red, and yellow as missiles flew towards the island and the deck cannons of the two destroyers thundered. Even from the distance the *Nightstalker* was from the island, Andy could hear the explosions. He imagined trees being blown apart, fires spreading throughout the island's jungles, and the buildings of the cultists being reduced to nothing more than rubble.

The barrage lasted until all the launchers and guns of the two ships had cycled through their ready payloads. When it was over, Captain Wall immediately ordered the weapons reloaded and a second strike.

It was difficult for Andy to focus on his job during the massive destruction that was taking place on the island and the booming of the ships' guns, but he did his best. As the second strike began, he picked up a large mass of contacts moving southward away from the island and passed on that data to fire control. Seconds later, shells splashed into the water at the location of the contacts and they were no more.

The second barrage on the island finally came to a stop. As it did so, Andy caught a glimpse of something odd on his screen.

Whatever it was, it was far too deep to be a mass of squids escaping the island. It registered as a single contact and not a mass of smaller ones. Its size sent a shiver along Andy's spine. Then, as fast as the contact had appeared, it was gone. He didn't have a chance to pass it along to fire control and frankly, he wasn't sure it would've mattered if he had. The contact had been so deep, there was very little that the two destroyers could have hit it with anyway. It had read as if it was on the very floor of the ocean.

Andy leaned back in his chair, rubbing his fingers over the bottom of his cheeks, wondering whether he not he should report it to Captain Wall. As fast as it had appeared and disappeared, it was easy to reason that the contact reading was nothing more than his own stressed-out mind playing a trick on him. Andy gave himself a few minutes before he made his choice on what to do. He decided to keep quiet about the contact and went back to listening to the captain and the others as they talked.

"Well, that's that." Captain Wall grinned. "Nothing on that island could've survived what we just threw at it."

"And we nailed the only group of squids trying to leave too," Franklin chimed in excitedly.

"Captain!" the comm. officer shouted. "The *Ares* is reporting she's under attack!"

****

Captain Lucas had put Lieutenant Jonathan Green in charge of the heightened security aboard the *Ares*. Jonathan didn't mind the job. He liked working with the ship's special response teams. Besides, it gave him a chance to carry an HK MP5 and feel like a real soldier. Jonathan enjoyed the feel of the loaded weapon in his hands. The *Ares* had a large stockpile of on-hand weapons for its special response teams. Some of them carried shotguns, other M-16s, Jonathan had even allowed one of the marines to break out a minigun from storage. What the heck, he thought, if we're guarding against real life monsters, it is better to be prepared than not.

Jonathan had the teams split up into groups of twos and threes patrolling the *Ares's* exterior decks and secondary two-man squads at her more vulnerable entrances. He figured it was overkill, but it was fun and the captain certainly wasn't going to call him on it.

Captain Lucas was freaked out and on edge over the squid creatures, like he had some kind of phobia of things with tentacles. Jonathan wasn't even sure he could bring himself to really believe the creatures existed without seeing one with his own eyes. He doubted too that the squids could be any real threat to the ship. Even if the squid creatures could move about on land, it didn't mean anything when it came to assaulting a state-of-the-art destroyer like the *Ares*.

Jonathan stood leaning over the railing of the ship's starboard side, looking out at the water. Night had fallen and the light of the moon was reflected on its surface. The evening was so calm and peaceful, it was hard to believe that the *Ares* and the *Nightstalker* had unleashed such a fury of destruction only minutes ago.

"Beautiful, ain't it?" Mark asked.

Jonathan turned to look at the marine. "Almost surreal after what we just watched."

"Tell me about it," Mark chuckled.

In the next instant, the top of Mark's head was gone. Something long and dark slashed through the air, cutting through bone and flesh. Mark's body flopped to the deck and lay there twitching.

Jonathan jerked around to see *something* standing only a few feet away from him. It stood on two, thick tentacles that supported the central mass of its body while other smaller tentacles, including the one that had killed Mark where he stood, writhed furiously about it.

Staring at the thing, Jonathan felt his bladder release itself. Warm trickles of urine flowed down his legs inside his pants. The creature took a swipe at him, one of its tentacles lashing outwards toward his chest. The tentacle made contact, swiping across him. Tiny bards shredded the cloth of his uniform and tore at his skin beneath it. Jonathan let out a yelp as he lost his balance and fell to land beside Mark's corpse. As a burning pain wracked his body, he cursed himself for not suiting up into full-combat gear like the teams he led. He had just been so busy and honestly hadn't expected any real action. Jonathan raised the barrel of his submachine gun, squeezing the weapon's trigger. It chattered as he sprayed the creature with a point-blank burst. One of the thing's tentacles was caught directly in his line of fire and was severed from the creature's body as the rest of the bullets pounded into the thing's body. The creature gave a shriek that made Jonathan think of a dying cat as it dove over the side railing and plunged into the water far below.

Hauling himself to his feet, Jonathan scrambled to peer over the side of the ship. His heart skipped a beat at what he saw there. Dozens of creatures like the one he had just faced were climbing up the side of the *Ares*. Each squid was using its main two tentacles to climb, slamming their spear-like tips into the armor of the hull and using them to propel themselves upwards much like ice climbers scaling a mountain.

Jonathan heard screams of warning ringing out from along the starboard side of the ship. They were followed quickly by the sound of gunfire. As all hell broke loose, Jonathan leaned over the side railing, pointing his weapon downward, and started blazing away the fast-approaching creatures. He swept his weapon back and forth, trying to hit as many of them as he could in hopes of knocking them loose from the side of the ship before they reached the deck he stood on.

It was clear the squids had been holding back as they increased their pace. With impossible speed, they moved up the sides of the ship like spiders. Jonathan had to abandon his position as the squids started to come over the railing and drop onto the deck all around him. One of the creatures tried to block the direction he ran in. He cut it to pieces with a quick burst and jumped over its still-flopping body as he sprinted toward the ship's main forward deck.

****

Captain Lucas covered his face with his hands. The gesture helped him to regain control of his raging emotions and focus his thoughts. The *Ares* was under attack, and it was his job to make sure she held firm and withstood it. He had ordered all her exterior entrances sealed, and the special reaction teams that guarded them to be redeployed to be available to deal with any breaches that occurred. Lucas had a clear view of the battle taking place on her main deck from the window of the bridge. It, like numerous other windows around the ship, couldn't be sealed. If the squids were strong enough to break through their reinforced glass, it would be up to the special reaction teams to keep the monsters out. And the squids were monsters. All his life, Lucas had been creeped out by cephalopods, and now he was living a personal nightmare come to life.

He had very little data on the squids. Their remaining numbers after the strike on the island were unknown. All he really knew about the things was that they were relentlessly aggressive, and they fed on living flesh. The ship's main weapon systems were useless with the monsters already aboard her. There would be no help coming from the other ships of DESRON 44. Putting assault boats into the water to come to her aid would be sentencing the soldiers aboard them to death. They would be overwhelmed long before they reached the *Ares*. He knew that Captain Wall was well aware of that fact as well.

Lucas recoiled from the bridge window in stark horror as a squid slammed its body against the glass in front of him. Its lesser tentacles whipped about, bashing into the glass over and over again as its primary two held it in place, wedged into the metal of the wall around the window. His XO, Gregory, caught him, keeping him on his feet.

"Are you okay, sir?" Gregory asked.

Lucas shook his head. "None of us are okay," he rasped, continuing to watch the squid outside hammer the bridge's window.

"Get a special reaction team up here ASAP. If that thing breaks through the glass…"

"Already done, sir," Gregory told him.

"I don't understand how they managed to sneak up on us like this to hit us out of the blue," Lucas commented. "How did we not see them coming?"

"I think sonar tech Hill has an answer for you there, sir," Gregory said and then shouted, "Hill, get over here!"

A young woman with bright red, regulation-cut hair and intense green eyes ran up to them. "Sir?" she asked.

"Tell Captain Lucas what you told me about the sonar," Gregory ordered her.

Hill nodded. "The electro-magnetic interference has increased, Captain Lucas. It knocked out my screen during the barrage on the island. I'm doing everything I can to get it back online, but it'll take time."

"And we still have no idea where this interference is coming from?" Lucas half-shouted at her, barely able to keep his frayed nerves in check.

"Not really, sir." Hill looked embarrassed as she answered. "I can tell you that these squid creatures themselves are emitting lesser but similar pulses of EMP to the one that is causing the issues with our comms and sonar."

"And you can't counter it somehow?" Lucas demanded.

"Like I said, sir, we're working on it," Hill assured him.

"Then why are you standing here?" Lucas snarled at her.

Hill blinked and then turned fully about, racing off towards her station.

Lucas noticed that Gregory was staring at him.

"What? You have something to say?" Lucas asked.

"Don't you think you were a tad harsh on her, sir?"

Lucas pointed at the squid outside the window.

"Take a look at that thing, Gregory! Working on it isn't a good enough answer. We need a solution and we need one now!"

"Agreed," Gregory said. "I am sure Captain Wall and the captains of DESRON 44 are aware of the problem with our sonar by now as well. Besides, sir, as you just pointed out, we have bigger issues than nonfunctional sonar screens to deal with."

****

Lieutenant Jonathan Green reached the *Ares's* main deck and joined the ever-tightening circle of soldiers trying to hold their ground there. The squids were coming at them from all sides. Whenever one died, it was as if two more scurried over the sides of the ship to replace them. The soldier he had allowed to carry a minigun was their saving grace. Spent shell casings flew from the weapon, clattering onto the deck, as the soldier's stream of fire cut through the squids like a scythe. Others fired into the ranks of the squids with shotguns and M-16s. Jonathan ejected an emptied magazine from his HK MP5 and reloaded. As soon as he slammed the fresh magazine home, he jerked up the submachine and added his fire to theirs.

"Sir!" one of the soldiers shouted at him. The soldier was pointing towards the horizon. Jonathan strained his eyes trying to make out what the soldier was trying to draw his attention to. Then Jonathan saw it. It was the helicopter from the *Nightstalker*. The bird was in route towards the *Ares*. She came in low and fast to take up a holding position above the ship's starboard side. Her side gunner's .50 caliber started blazing away at the squids. Cheers went up from the circle of soldiers around Jonathan, and for the first time, Jonathan allowed himself to believe that they all weren't going to be massacred by the squids' superior numbers.

Those same cheers turned to cries of terror as the helicopter came under attack. The squids that were clambering up the sides of the *Ares* began to hurl themselves skyward towards the copter as they reached the top of her starboard side instead of simply toppling over the railing onto her deck. The incredible strength of the squids' two primary tentacles sent the creatures vaulting into the air. Most of the creatures missed their target, either careening to land in splattered masses on the deck or to splash into the water around the ship. Those that hit though dug into the bottom of the copter, their two larger tentacles spearing its body and keeping them attached to it. The few squids that reached the copter scampered over it like spiders. The gunner in the copter's side door couldn't bring his .50 caliber around at an angle sharp enough to target the monsters.

Jonathan could see the other soldiers in the helicopter's rear compartment trying to bring their personal weapons to bear on the monsters. M-16 barrels flashed in the darkness of the night. It wasn't enough though. A squid speared one of the soldiers trying to cover the bird's gunner and entrance and dragged the man out into the open air. Blood flew as the soldier slid from the tip of the squid's tentacle and fell into the water. Jonathan lost sight of the man as he dropped below his line of sight, but Jonathan could imagine what awaited the soldier there—a sea churning with hungry squids ready to feast upon him.

The gunner behind the helicopter's .50 caliber died next as a squid darted inside the rear compartment over him, flinging him out in the process. The gunner's body twisted through the air as it plunged downwards.

Jonathan was forced to tear his gaze away from the helicopter's plight as a squid broke its way into the circle of soldiers on the *Ares*'s deck and came shrieking towards him. He peppered it with rounds from his submachine gun, sending sprays of black blood splashing outward from where the bullets pierced its body. Even before the creature skidded to a stop, dead, at his feet, Jonathan turned his attention to the helicopter again. It was spinning out of control, and Jonathan could see the pilot wrestling with one of the squids through the bird's forward window.

"Get down!" Jonathan shouted at the men around him as the helicopter descended to crash into the *Ares*'s starboard side. It struck one of the cannons there dead on. The helicopter and a good portion of the ship vanished in a burst of heat and flames before setting off a series of secondary explosions that ran the length of the *Ares*. Jonathan screamed as his flesh was cooked alive on his bones and his uniform was burnt away.

****

Captain Lucas was screaming as the bits of the squid outside the bridge's main window came flying inward accompanied by a rain of shattered glass. The glass shards flew like tiny daggers slicing their way through those closest to the bridge's window. His XO, Gregory, took several shards to his arms and chest, but it was the one that buried itself in his right eye that killed him. Gregory's already-dead body careened backwards to crash into the bridge's wall and slid down it to the floor.

Pain shot through Lucas as bits of the window's glass slashed grooves in the skin of his cheek. Others cut at his arms and legs as he threw himself behind the sonar station. Sonar Tech Hill sat in her chair above him where he crouched on the floor. She made horrid gargling noises as her hands vainly groped for the large shard of glass that protruded from the middle of her neck. Her eyes were wide as Lucas looked, helplessly, up into them.

Lucas heard the soldiers of the special reaction team on the bridge opening fire and knew the squids were coming through the broken window. The *Ares*'s deck shook under him as explosions continued to ripple through her.

"Damage report!" he shouted, getting to his feet, but there was no one to answer him. Most of the bridge crew was dead and the special reaction team had their hands full trying to hold the squids swarming through the bridge window at bay.

Lucas staggered to the communications station and flicked on the ship's intercom as he picked up the ready mic there. "All hands, this Captain Lucas. Abandon ship! I repeat, abandon ship!"

Those were words Captain Lucas had never thought he would say. The *Ares* had survived numerous engagements over the years with very little damage. It was cold comfort to think it had taken monsters to end her.

"Captain Lucas!" the leader of the special reaction team yelled at him. "We need to get you out of here, sir!"

Lucas thought he remembered the officer's name being Cortez. He wore the rank of a marine corporal on his uniform. Lucas allowed Cortez to take him by the arm and drag him from the mess the bridge had become. The floors were slicked with both human and squid blood as Cortez led him into the corridor beyond it.

There had been four men on Cortez's team including Cortez himself. It took Lucas a moment to notice that only one of them was left accompanying himself and the corporal from the bridge. Cortez yanked his sidearm from the holster on his hip and pressed it into Lucas's hand. Lucas accepted the pistol with a nod of thanks.

"Figure you might need that, sir," Cortez shouted over the barking chatter of his M-16 as he dispatched a squid stupid enough to try to follow them into the corridor.

Lucas readied his pistol. It had been a long, long time since he had needed a weapon in his own hand. Navy captains commanded from the bridge, not from the trenches. Lucas had no idea what Cortez hoped to achieve by running or where the corporal was taking him to. It didn't take a captain to know that most of the *Ares* was fire and the ship was on her way to rest beneath the waves.

****

Colonel Brannon Jackson was glad he refused to let his Reapers be a part of the attempt to aid the *Ares*. The helicopter and all the troops aboard it that Captain Wall had dispatched were nothing more than memories. Brannon wouldn't have believed the squids could take out an assault copter had he not witnessed it with his own eyes from the bridge of the *Nightstalker*. His decision to hold back his Reapers from the attempt to help the *Ares* had been made because his men needed time to recover after the disastrous raid on the island, not from fear of the squids. They had all been itching to go though. It had taken a lot to keep them off the copter when it had lifted from the *Nightstalker's* helipad.

The *Ares* was adrift and slowly sinking as she continued to light the night with the fires that burned along her entire length. Every once in a while, a new round of explosions would erupt as the flames reached fresh ammo storage compartments or fuel tanks aboard her.

Captain Wall had ordered the other ships of DESRON 44 into motion. The *Nightstalker* and the three frigates were pushing their engines to give the *Ares* as wide a berth as possible as they pulled away from her flaming wreckage.

The water around the *Ares* was thick with squids. The creatures easily still numbered in the hundreds. Brannon didn't want to think about how so many of the creatures were left alive after how the DESRON's two destroyers had hammered the island.

Malcom stood behind him on the *Nightstalker's* bridge, scratching at the top of his head, and muttering something about the devils in the water. Adam, Vander, and Zahn were there with him.

Captain Wall and her XO stood at the bridge's forward window watching the *Ares* sink even as the *Nightstalker* angled away from her, heading northward. Brannon knew the order Captain Wall was about to give before she spoke it.

"Franklin," she said sadly. "Take the *Ares* with guns."

The XO nodded, frowning himself. "Yes, ma'am."

The idea, Brannon knew, was to eliminate as many of the remaining squids around the *Ares* as possible by hopefully causing the sinking ship to detonate entirely. The nukes about it wouldn't go off no matter how hard the *Nightstalker* hit her, but whatever was left of the more conventional missiles and arms aboard her would. The ensuing blast would catch the squids gathered around the sinking ship within it, sending the creatures back to whatever Hell they had scampered out of to begin with. The bad part was that if there were any survivors alive aboard the ship, they would get toasted right along with the squids. It was a tough call to make and he respected Wall's ability to do it.

Brannon was beyond thinking of the squids as manmade, biological weapons of mass destruction at this point. He thought of the things as demons. He didn't know if it was his faith or the horror films and novels that Vander had exposed him to over the years they had known each other, but demons was the best term to describe the squids by as far as Brannon was concerned.

Missiles flew from the *Nightstalker*'s launchers to streak down on the burning wreckage of the *Ares*. The already massively damaged destroyer shuddered and broke apart in a blossoming ball of orange and red light, the heat from the blast boiling the water around her.

"Patch me through to the rest ships of DESRON 44," Captain Wall barked at her communications officer.

"You're on, ma'am," a brown-haired ensign with thick glasses told her.

"This is COMDESRON 44. All ships disengage from hostiles and follow the *Nightstalker*'s heading. We're getting the Hell out of here," Captain Wall's voice boomed over the open frequency. As yet, the DESRON's short-range communications had been crippled by the sporadic EMP interference like its long-range comm. had been.

Brannon wasn't a Navy officer but he had overheard enough talk on the *Nightstalker's* bridge to know that the same EMP interference had played havoc with the DESRON's sonar too. From what he gathered, that issue had been dealt with though, at least to an extent. He felt better knowing that the DESRON wasn't running blind. He wasn't fool enough either to think that if any squids were alive that the creatures were going to let the remainder of the DESRON escape without another fight.

"Captain Wall," Brannon called out.

"What is it, Colonel?" Wall snapped, whirling around to face him. "You may not have noticed, but I am a little busy right now."

"I just wanted to say that you made the right call in regards to the *Ares,* ma'am."

Wall's expression softened. Brannon knew how he would have felt in her place if he had been the one to open fire on one of his own ships.

"Thank you," she said, professional demeanor cracking if only for an instant.

****

The ships of DESRON 44 had left the island behind. There had been no other attack by the squids or sign of the creatures for over an hour. Things aboard the *Nightstalker* were beginning to return to as close to normal as they could under the circumstances. Captain Wall had called for a meeting of the DESRON's captains via video comms in her office at oh-three-hundred hours. She had invited Colonel Brannon to join them. Brannon wasn't overly excited about doing so but thought it wise to stay as inside the command loop as he could. Technically, with the raid on the island concluded, he wasn't part of the DESRON's chain of command at all.

Brannon arrived at Wall's office a few minutes early to find Wall sitting alone behind her desk. There was an open bottle of Vodka on it beside two full shot glasses. Wall smiled at him as he entered.

"Take a seat, Colonel," she ordered him. "We've got a few minutes before things get started."

He could see she already had her laptop rigged up for the video conference as she handed him one of the shot glasses.

"To the good men and women who gave their lives for us today," she said, raising her own glass to down its contents in a single slug.

Brannon didn't drink, but in this situation, to not do so would be insulting, so he took a sip from his glass before placing it back on top of Captain Wall's desk.

"It was a hard day by anyone's standards, ma'am," he said.

Captain Wall poured another glass of Vodka for herself and then glanced at the watch on her wrist. "We have ten minutes or so left until we're on duty again, Colonel, so please, call me Sarah."

"Thank you, Sarah," he said with a smile spreading across his lips.

"What you said to me on the bridge today … that meant a lot. I'm the one who should be thanking you."

"I get it," Brannon told her. "It's never easy to make that sort of call but sometimes it has to be done … and it did today."

Wall nodded and changed the subject. "Lieutenant Sharps was a close friend of mine. It was hard for me not to hate you for what happened on the island. I am human despite the rumor to the contrary."

"Glad you don't." Brannon's smile grew wider. "And if you think you're a cold one, you should meet my man, Vander. Sometimes I think the guy died a long time ago and reanimated as a zombie with sniper skills. Unless it's about comic books or SF stuff, I swear I have never seen the man get emotional about anything."

"Comic books, really?" Wall asked.

"To each, their own I guess." Brannon shrugged.

Brannon politely took another sip of his Vodka as Wall finished her second.

"I have to ask though, Sarah, why did you invite me to this meeting? With the raid on the island done, this is your show now."

"I'd be a fool to waste an asset such as you, Brannon. I've read over the parts of your record that aren't classified above my clearance level. Frankly, you've lived through stuff that should have been impossible to make it out alive from."

"And you're facing the impossible now." Brannon leaned forward in his chair. "We didn't finish the squids even when we blew up the *Ares,* did we?"

"No," Wall admitted. "According to the latest sonar sweeps, there are a good number of the creatures on our heels. Not enough I think to be a threat to the DESRON…"

"But if they all came at a single ship again," Brannon finished for her, "that could mean another round of real trouble."

"Exactly," Wall confirmed. "I have thought of sending some torpedoes their way, but based on what we've seen so far, I highly doubt it would scare them off. They're determined little monsters. That's for sure. And they aren't clustered close enough together to even stand a chance of doing any real damage to their numbers."

"So what *is* the plan?" Brannon asked.

"That's why we are having this meeting, Brannon," Wall told him. "To hopefully come up with one because at this point, I have nothing."

****

The screen of Wall's laptop came to life with an image of the DESRON's three commanders aboard their respective frigates. Commander Troy Daniels, of the USS *Blackthorn,* was a young man in his early twenties, but Brannon judged him a component from his composure. Commander Bethany Davis, the USS *Smith,* struck him as being a decent officer as well, if a seemingly inexperienced one. She appeared to be even younger than Daniels was. Commander Sam Ringo though was the kind of knuckle-head CO that got people killed. Brannon had seen enough officers like him over the years to peg him as one the moment he spoke.

"What is the meaning of this meeting, ma'am?" Ringo demanded of Wall in spite of his lesser rank. "There hasn't been any sign of the squids other than random clusters since we began northward."

Wall ignored Ringo's demand for an explanation and got to business.

"I've called you all here because regardless of opinions to the contrary, we are being followed. It's true the squids appear to lack the numbers to be a threat to DESRON 44, as a whole, but any one of our ships could come under attack before we are able to keep our planned rendezvous with DESRON 12. We need a plan for dealing with such an engagement if should occur, people, plain and simple."

"I think we've already done all we can in that regard, ma'am," Commander Daniels said.

"Agreed," Commander Ringo nodded. "Beyond establishing armed patrols of our decks and sealing off the entrances to the interiors of our ships, what else can we do?"

"I suppose the answer is not much," Commander Davis sighed. "Unless you have something else in mind, Captain Wall?"

"I don't," Wall answered.

Brannon cleared his throat to get Captain Wall's attention.

"Colonel?" She turned to look at him. "You have something else in mind?"

"I do." Brannon nodded. "I believe the armed patrols you have on yours decks are a great start, but you can do more in that regard. The primary weapon systems of your ships aren't designed to protect her against boarders. In this day and age, if the enemy is able to board you, it usually means you're dead already."

Captain Wall and the others were nodding.

"However, you all have stores of weapons aboard your ships that include miniguns and SAWs. I recommend setting up gun emplacements at intervals all along the decks. They will not only add to your firepower in terms of stopping the squids from boarding but can be redirected to engage the squids if and when they do make it aboard your decks."

"That's a good idea." Commander Davis smiled.

"I want those emplacements set up on every ship in the DESRON within the hour," Wall ordered.

"Ma'am," Ringo spoke up. "The squids may not be grouped tightly enough for us to truly engage them with our primary weapon systems at this point, but I still suggest that we make use of what have. A few torpedoes spent on keeping them distant from the body of the DESRON might save our lives on down the line."

Captain Wall sighed. "I've already considered that, Commander Ringo. I remain hesitant to expend munitions that we may need later for such little effect."

"Little effect?" Ringo challenged her. "Any squids we take out we won't have to deal with if they do opt to engage us, and I can't see any reason to hold back. DESRON 12 is not that far away in the grand scheme of things. Also, it's possible that a few such strikes might drive the squids trailing away when they learn we are not the easy prey that they likely hope we are."

Wall openly laughed. "Commander, those things aren't going to let us go no matter what we do. Surely you can see that by now. They were created to be relentless and certainly excel at being so."

"Have we been able to learn anything about them or the EM interference that's been playing havoc with our comms and sonar?" Daniels asked.

"Actually, we have," Wall admitted.

Brannon blinked in surprise, wondering why Captain Wall hadn't already shared whatever new intel she had.

"The drive Colonel Jackson retrieved from the cultists' compound on the island had more information about the squids within its data than we originally believed. The EM interference we have been experiencing is from the squids themselves."

"What?" Commander Ringo blurted out. "That's impossible!"

"No, it isn't," Commander Daniels piped up. "I've heard of oceanic lifeforms that emit EM waves before and what the captain is saying makes perfect sense if you stop to consider we didn't have the issues with our equipment until we came in close range of the squids. That interference has lessened as well with the decreased number of squids left alive."

"Lessened, yes," Commander Davis cut in, "but not enough to account for the amount of squids we have destroyed. The number trailing us is nothing compared to what was on that island. If we're really saying the squids are the cause, the EM interference should be almost nonexistent now."

Commander Daniels gave a shrug. "She has a point, but I still believe the squids themselves are somehow the source of our tech problems."

"Could be there's something out there causing the EM that we haven't seen yet," Brannon suggested.

"What do you mean by that?" Commander Ringo snapped.

"I meant exactly what I said, Commander," Brannon stared, unflinching at the older man.

"Let's table the discussion of the interference for the time being," Captain Wall told them all. "The state of our sonar has improved drastically and while long-range comms would be nice, they are going to make the difference in keeping us alive. We need to keep our focus on that."

No one argued with Wall's assessment of the situation.

Nothing else of importance was established in the meeting before it ended, beyond Captain Wall giving the order for the DESRON to increase its speed towards the scheduled rendezvous with DESRON 12. Captain Wall closed her laptop as she shot Brannon a questioning look.

"What was all that about?" she asked. "Do you really believe there's something else out there?"

Brannon chuckled. "You would think flesh-eating squids that move about on land would be enough, right?"

"Seriously, Colonel, what did you mean?"

Brannon noticed that though the other commands were no longer with them via video/audio link, that she addressed him by his rank and not his name.

"The interference you're facing has to come from somewhere, and if the squids are indeed the source, then either there is a lot more of them out there than any of us care to imagine, or there's something else that we haven't seen yet causing it."

Captain Wall stared at him, waiting for him to explain more about his theory.

Brannon sighed. "The cultists believed there was a giant monster asleep on the floor of the ocean in this region, right?"

Wall nodded.

"But they never found it," Brannon said. "They created all these smaller creatures, we think, to take its place in their plans."

Brannon leaned forward. "What if they were right about the giant one all along and just never stumbled onto it?"

"And now it's awake and after us?" Wall frowned.

"We did blow the heck out of that island. What we did there was enough to wake up anything by standards," Brannon told her.

"Let's assume you're right." Wall cracked her knuckles. "Then what is this creature and what does it want?"

"You got me," Brannon shrugged. "I'm not an expert on the occult or a scientist either. I can assure you of one thing though, and that is that this creature, whatever it may be, has the same goal as the squids we've encountered."

"To feed and kill whatever it comes across," Wall said.

"Yes, ma'am," Brannon confirmed.

****

Vander was kicked back on the top bunk bed of the quarters he, Malcom, and Adam had been assigned aboard the *Nightstalker*. He flipped half-heartedly through the pages of the comic he was reading on his tablet.

Malcom was stretched out on the bunk across from Vander's, trying to get some sleep. That wasn't happening for him though because Adam kept pacing the length of the room. The sound of his heavy boots on the metal was distracting to Vander and Malcom alike. Malcom's time in quarantine had been a short one. The doctors on the *Nightstalker* had run a slew of tests and workups both on him and the squid blood that had stained the combat gear he had worn onto the island. All of them checked out as clear of biological hazards. As thus, he had been freed from sickbay and allowed to rejoin the others.

"Relax, man," Vander urged Adam. "We're not on the sharp end anymore, okay?"

Adam paused to stare up at him. Vander swore he heard Adam actually growl at him but ignored it.

"You're wound up too tight, buddy." Vander sat down his tablet. "You keep going like this and you will snap."

"He snapped a long time ago, Vander," Malcom grumbled pulling his pillow further up over his head.

"Frag you," Adam muttered. "At least I'm not a coward, Root."

Malcom flung his pillow aside and sat up so fast in his bed that he nearly banged his head on the bottom of the bunk above him. "I am not a coward."

Adam snorted. "Sure could've fooled me."

"I think you both need to chill out." Vander slid down from the top bunk he sat on, his boots thudding against the metal of the floor.

Adam whirled on him. "You got a problem, ice man?"

"Oh, you so did not just call me that." Vander gritted his teeth. "That's pretty insulting, Adam, even coming from someone as ignorant of fine literature as you are."

"My issue is with Root, not you, cold boy," Adam snarled. "I'm sick of being ordered around by a soldier whose head isn't even fully in the game anymore."

Malcom slid out of his bunk, getting to his feet. "Careful," he warned.

"Mate, Malcom did just fine on that island, if you ask me." Vander flashed his white teeth at Adam.

"I didn't ask you, did I?" Adam snapped. "I was talking to our resident coward."

"I am not a coward," Malcom said again, his hands clinching into fists where they hung at his sides.

"Whatever you want to call it then, sir." Adam made the last word sound like an insult. "You're too focused on saving your own butt and seeing that family of yours again. You've lost your edge. You don't get your head straight, we're all gonna pay the price for it."

"This from the poster child for PTSD?" Malcom waved a hand in Adam's direction then continued. "You're the one hanging on by a thread, Adam, whether you want to admit it or not. Your wife dying really messed you over."

"Don't you talk about her." Adam took a step towards Malcom.

Vander moved to stand between them. "We've all got issues. Drop this now before one of you does something we'll all regret."

Vander's voice was so cold the temperature in the room seemed to dip as he spoke. Neither Adam nor Malcom failed to notice that the fingers of Vander's right hand flexed where they hung near the handle of the knife sheathed on his belt.

The door to their quarters opened as Brannon entered with the newest member of the Reapers, Zahn, in tow. He looked from one of them to the next, appraising each of them in turn. "Something going on here I should know about?"

"No, sir!" Vander said, snapping to attention. "We're all good, Colonel."

"That's fantastic," Brannon quipped, clearly not believing Vander. "Because I have got a job for the lot of you slackers."

****

Franklin stood staring through the main forward window of the *Nightstalker's* bridge. His hands were clasped behind his back. He was happy to take this watch. Captain Wall had needed rest badly and it had taken all he could do to convince her to finally try and get some sleep. The sun was high in the sky as the *Nightstalker* raced through the water. Her engines weren't pushed to their maximum but they were close. Captain Wall wanted to reach DESRON 12 as fast as possible and Franklin couldn't blame her for that. He hadn't been a part of the earlier meeting, but Wall had informed him of Colonel Jackson's suspicion that something worse than the squids could be out there creeping up on the ships of DESRON 44. That was why he wasn't as surprised as he might have been otherwise when Sonar Tech Carter started shouting for him.

"Surface contact!" Carter yelled. "It's CBDR, sir!"

"Where from?"

"Whatever it is, it's closing fast from the south, sir."

"What do you mean whatever it is?" Franklin demanded.

"It's huge, sir, larger than a battle carrier."

Franklin's eyes bugged as he moved to where Carter sat and took a look over the tech's shoulder at the sonar screen. "It's moving at forty knots?" Franklin stammered.

"Yes, sir!" Carter said. "Forty knots. It will reach DESRON 44 in five minutes, sir!"

"Nothing that large can move that fast," Franklin protested the data his eyes were scanning over.

Sonar Tech Andy Carter wisely kept silent as Franklin stopped leaning over him and stood fully upright once more.

Franklin returned to the center of the bridge as he started barking orders. "Somebody get Captain Wall up here ASAP. Comms, try to hail whatever that thing out there approaching is. We need to make sure it's not some off-chart cruise liner or assistance we weren't told was coming!"

An ensign darted from the bridge to fetch the captain as the comm officer told Franklin, "It's not returning our hails, sir!"

"Keep trying," Franklin told her and turned his attention towards the sonar station again. "Carter! What can you tell me about it?"

"I believe the contact is biological in nature, sir! The way it's moving through the water..." Carter's explanation died on his lips as his expression became even more panicked. He spun in his chair back towards the controls of his station and his fingers danced over them with experienced speed.

"Sir!" Carter half screamed. "We've lost sonar!"

"Comms are out too!" Franklin heard from the opposite side of the bridge.

He lifted his arms into the air, interlocking his fingers behind his neck, to flex their muscles. Captain Wall had given the order for the ship's CIWS to remain active. The system's gun came to life, opening fire at the still distant but quickly approaching contact.

A virtual wall of bullets flew over the waves towards the horizon. Franklin strained trying to see what the automated system was targeting but there was nothing there. Whatever it was, it had to be below the water line. That meant the fire of the CIWS was useless. He wondered if the CIWS was glitching out like so many other systems aboard the *Nightstalker* were.

Franklin breathed a sigh of relief as he saw Captain Wall step onto the bridge. She looked haggard and blurry eyed, her uniform ruffled and its shirt buttoned crookedly. None the less, he was very thankful to see her.

"Captain on the bridge!" he yelled and surrendered his command to her.

"You're relieved," she acknowledged him and hurried to take her seat in the bridge's command chair. "Status?"

"Unknown contact approaching from the south. CBDR at forty knots. ETA in three minutes," Franklin informed her then added, "Comms and sonar are cutting in and out."

Captain Wall plopped into her seat. "Increased EM interference?"

"Yes, ma'am. We believe its source is the biologic approaching us."

"Take contact with guns," Wall showed her teeth, "and blow whatever it is to Hell."

"Taking contact with guns," Franklin said, glancing at the weapons officer.

Two Mark 50 torpedoes fired from the *Nightstalker*. They swam through the waves like high-speed sharks in route towards their target.

"Torpedo contact in three ... two ... one," the weapons officer called out and then shouted, "Contact!"

Water sprayed skyward from beneath the waves where the torpedoes had struck.

"Direct hit by both, ma'am," Carter confirmed, thankful the sonar was online again for the moment. He had done his best to jury rig shielding for it to protect the sensitive equipment from the EM interference whatever was out there was putting off. The contact changed course in the wake of the underwater explosions. "Contact is veering away from DESRON 44!"

Officers and crewmen were cheering all over the bridge. Captain Wall and her XO exchanged a serious look. They both knew that whatever they had just hit was still out there and very much alive. Carter hadn't reported it, but she guessed the contact hadn't even slowed down as it shifted its heading.

"Let's not get cocky people," Captain Wall warned her bridge crew. "We might have scared whatever is out there away for the moment, but you can bet it'll be back."

"It already is, ma'am," Sonar Tech Andy Carter's voice cut the new fallen silence on the bridge.

****

Commander Bethany Davis watched in horror as the USS *Blackthorn died.* The massive surface contact that Captain Wall, aboard the *Nightstalker*, had seemed to drive off veered around at impossible speed. She was sure the crew of the *Blackthorn* hadn't had time to do anything more than see death coming for them. The contact rammed into the *Blackthorn*, below the waterline, and the force of the impact broke the ship in two.

That was far from the worst of it though. No matter how long she lived, Bethany Davis knew she would never forget the glimpse she caught of the tentacles that shot up out of the water to grab the two halves of the broken frigate, wrap around them, and drag them below the waves. The tentacles were so large she could clearly see the suckers of each even across the distance between her ship, the *Smith,* and where the monster writhed beneath the waves.

"Evasive maneuvers!" Davis screamed at her crew. "Engines at full. I want us out of here before that comes after us too!"

"Yes, ma'am!" her XO answered, moving to make sure her orders were carried out.

Davis slumped down into her command chair. There was no hope of outrunning that *thing* out there in the water if it did come after them, but she would be damned if she was going to sit back and do nothing. She couldn't explain why her reaction had been to run. Maybe it was some sort of primal fear that instinctually took her over. Adrenaline was surging through her as her mind continued to race. Her mind was unable to rationally process what it had just witnessed.

"Joseph!" she barked at her sonar tech. "Where is that thing now?"

He turned to her, looking just as terrified as she felt. "I don't know, ma'am. It's vanished from my screen."

"Find it!" Davis shouted. "We don't have the time for screw ups right now."

"Ma'am," her XO, Watson, was suddenly at her side. "Captain Wall has ordered the ships of the DESRON to scatter and make a run for it."

"We're already doing that," Davis snapped, exasperated.

Watson took a step back at the fury in her voice.

"Ma'am! I have the contact on my screen again. The *Martin* has taken it with guns," her sonar tech informed her.

"What the Hell does Ringo think he's doing?" Davis muttered.

Watson must have overheard her because he said, "I don't know, ma'am, but if Ringo wants to be fool enough to engage that thing, it just buys us more time."

"That's pretty cold," Davis said with a slight grin, looking over at Watson.

"True though," Watson replied without flinching.

"I'm reading multiple torpedo impacts in the water!" her sonar tech shouted. "If they had any effect on the contact, ma'am, I'm not seeing it."

"The *Nightstalker* has been forced into a southward heading," Watson told her. "Wall's burning up her engines getting out of here."

"Let's do the same," Davis ordered. "Push them past the redline."

"Yes, ma'am," Watson nodded, though it was clear he thought that it was a bad idea. Perhaps he was right in a sense. If they damaged the engines in their headlong flight out of the area, they would be a sitting duck later on if that thing followed them and not the *Nightstalker*. Right now, she didn't care though. If they haul butt out of here, they wouldn't be around later to worry about the engines or anything else.

"The *Martin* is hammering that thing with everything they have," Watson commented.

Davis could hear the distant explosions taking place to the *Smith's* rear. She hoped like Hell that Ringo was hurting that thing, and bad. Based on what she imagined its size must be, it wasn't going to be an easy kill by anyone's standards. It was flesh and blood, however, and that meant it could bleed and die.

The explosions stopped all at once. After a moment of silence, a single, terrifyingly large explosion rippled across the waves. Davis lurched forward in her chair as if the *Smith* itself had been struck. The shockwaves had pounded into her hull, rocking the ship in the water. Davis's gut felt like it was full of razors and a sheen of sweat glistened on her skin.

"That was the *Martin* going up, Captain," Watson told her. "Our aft lookouts report that the squid rose up from the water and embraced it, crushing the ship to itself. The pressure must have detonated the *Martin's* onboard munitions."

"Ringo's dead?" Davis asked her eyes wide. She hated the man, but he was still a human being, not to mention his poor crew.

"Has to be, ma'am," Watson nodded. "No one could have survived what the lookouts reported they saw."

"And the squid?" Davis said allowing herself to call the thing out there what it was.

"It's CBDR, ma'am!" her sonar tech yelped. She had never heard anyone so panicked.

"ETA, thirty seconds!" the tech added.

"Fire aft torpedoes!" Davis wailed.

"At this range…" Watson started.

"Fire!" Davis screamed again.

The *Smith's* aft launchers spat a volley of torpedoes into the water. They streaked towards their target. It was so close they didn't have to travel far. The ensuing explosion rocked the *Smith*.

"Damage report!" Davis demanded. She never got an answer. The whole bridge was filled with screams as Davis looked up and saw the sun streaming in through the *Smith's* forward window, blocked by an enormous tentacle descending upon it. The tentacle smacked into the ship. Metal creaked and squealed as it folded inward. Davis was flung from her chair by the tentacle's impact. When she regained her senses enough to see what was happening around her, she knew they were all dead. The bodies of several members of her bridge crew were scattered about. Most had broken bones from bouncing off their consoles or being tossed about into the walls of the bridge. Those that weren't hurt were desperately trying to help the wounded. No one was at their stations, not that it mattered. The ship's power had gone dead. Fires raged and flickered in the chaos where equipment had blown out. Wires dangled from a section of the collapsed roof on the bridge.

Davis whipped her head about looking for Watson. Her XO's corpse rested in a pool of his own blood only a few feet from where she lay. A jagged piece of metal impaled Watson, running completely through his chest and into the floor below him.

The tentacle still blocked the sun. She imagined it was wrapped around the *Smith* much like it had done to the wreckage of the

Martin. More stations were blowing out and the bridge's roof was getting closer and closer to its floor as the tentacle continued to apply pressure to the ship's structure. The tentacle suddenly recoiled, leaving the smashed bridge window open.

The water took her by surprise when it came rushing onto the bridge. Commander Bethany Davis tried to scream, but the rushing water silenced her. It shoved its way down her throat through her open mouth and into her lungs. Her last thought was of her home in Idaho and the horses there she would never see again.

****

"I regret to inform you captain that we have lost the *Blackthorn,* the *Smith,* and the *Martin,*" Franklin told her. It was clear from the tone of his voice that he was feeling the shock that she felt herself. A giant monster like something from a horror movie had just torn DESRON 44 to shreds in matter of minutes. Her ship, the *Nightstalker,* was now the sole survivor of the DESRON.

"And the monster?" she asked as she noticed Colonel Jackson watching her intently.

"It's gone deep, ma'am," Franklin replied. "Mr. Carter says its last course was in a direction away from us."

"As fast as that thing is, it doesn't matter," Wall chuckled darkly. "The head-start we have won't be enough to save us."

"Our engines are running beyond their recommended safety protocols already," Franklin reminded her. "There's nothing more we can squeeze out of them."

"I know." Wall sighed. "I hate running, but it seems like our only option."

"We could fight, ma'am," Franklin suggested.

"Don't be an idiot, man," Brannon cut in. The colonel looked as if he was about to put Franklin on the floor of the bridge. "Your Commander Ringo tried that. The *Smith* got off a couple of shots too. Neither of them did anything more than make that thing out there angrier."

"We all know that thing is coming for us next. Our long-range communications are still down," Franklin snarled at Brannon. "What other option do we have, Colonel? You've seen how fast that thing moves in the water."

"That's exactly my point." Brannon met Franklin's eyes. "We need to get out of the water."

"The island." Wall perked up in her command chair.

Brannon nodded. "We may have blown the Hell out that place, but it's still there."

"That island could still be crawling with those little versions of that bastard thing out there," Franklin protested.

"Any port in a storm." Wall grinned. "That's something we'll have to take our chances on."

"You're assuming we can make there, ma'am," Franklin said. "That monster already wants us dead. How do you think it's going to feel about us returning to the place where we killed its children?"

"There's no connection between the little ones and that bad boy out there," Brannon pointed out. "At least not that we know of. Why would you call the little ones its children?"

"It just seems to fit," Franklin explained.

Brannon thought it over for a second. "Could be you're right. I saw the ones on that island up close and personal. They sure do look a lot like that thing out there."

"This speculation is pointless, gentlemen," Wall interrupted.

Franklin and Brannon both fell silent staring at her.

"What matters are reaching the island and what we do when we get there." Wall got up from her command chair and stood up straight. "If we make it, we won't have much time to abandon ship and to get whatever we can in terms of supplies onto land."

"I'll start organizing a list of what we'll need most and the manpower to move it over as quickly as possible." Franklin started to race away.

"Franklin," Wall stopped him. "Make weapons a priority. As you pointed out, we have no idea if the island is fully cleared or not."

"Yes, ma'am," he answered and then turned away, barking orders at the other officers on the bridge.

"You really think this is a good idea?" Wall whispered to Brannon.

"It's the best shot of living through this mess that we have." He shrugged. "I'll let my boys know what's happening and get them ready."

****

"You're freaking kidding me!" Malcom raged.

"Wish I was," Brannon shrugged.

"That thing out there really destroyed the entire DESRON?" Vander asked, his ice-cold voice cracking for the first time in Brannon's memory. Brannon watched Vander catch himself and force his air of usual aloofness back onto his face.

"Sure did." Brannon kept packing up his gear as the other Reapers did the same. "The *Nightstalker* is all that's left."

Adam grunted but gave no other comment on the matter. Instead, he picked up his rifle from where it lay on his bunk and checked its magazine.

Malcom was not holding up well. Brannon couldn't blame him. Not long ago at all, they all thought they were safe and on route for home. He knew how much Malcom's family meant to him and how determined he was to see them again. The situation was rough enough without having that type of personal pressure added to the mix. Brannon knew he couldn't fully grasp what Malcom was going through. He didn't really have any family of his own to speak of. This squad, his squad, was his family. Assuring Malcom they were going to be okay wasn't going to work. Malcom was just as much a veteran of SNAFU stuff as he was and knew the odds weren't in their favor on living through this one.

"That island is a deathtrap," Malcom snarled. "I can't believe we're headed onto it again."

Brannon settled for simply saying, "It could be worse, Malcom."

"You guys sure live up to your reputation," Zahn laughed.

"Oh, and what's our rep, newb?" Malcom snapped.

"You really are like some kind of suicide squad," Zahn laughed.

"There is nothing funny about this mess, Zahn," Malcom scowled and started towards Zahn.

Brannon stepped into his path, blocking him. Malcom threw his arms in the air, disgusted, and went back to packing his gear. Brannon shot Zahn a cautionary look of warning.

"We're all wound a bit tight right now," Brannon said. "Just keep in mind that's better than being dead."

Vander raised a hand like he was a kid in school waiting on Brannon to call on him.

"What is it, Vander?" Brannon asked.

"If we're the Suicide Squad, does that mean Adam is Harley Quinn?" Vander snorted.

Adam growled in Vander's direction. Brannon thanked God that Adam didn't do more.

"Stow it, Vander," Brannon ordered.

"Sure thing, boss, I call dibs on being Deadshot though."
Vander smiled and gave his customized M24 an overly dramatic
kiss on its barrel. Brannon did his best to ignore the gesture but
found himself smirking anyway before he settled back down to the
business at hand. He noticed that Adam was already ready to roll
and decided to take advantage of the moment.

"Adam, a word," Brannon said, motioning for Adam to join him
in the corridor outside the room.

Adam followed him out and Brannon shut the door behind
them. His gut told him he had finally stumbled on how to deal with
the ready-to-snap soldier. Malcom was falling apart too, yes, but
Adam was a time bomb waiting to explode.

"What do you need, Colonel?" Adam asked. "You want me to
tell you I'm fine? Well, I'm not. I'm not scared to tears like that
baby Malcom in there, but I know I ain't right either. I ain't been
right for a long time now."

Brannon smiled. "Thanks for being honest with me."

"Ah heck, Colonel, you knew. I've seen you watching me,
waiting for me to lose it."

"I have faith in you," Brannon lied, feigning a smile as he
reached out to put a hand on Adam's shoulder. "I've got a job for
you too."

Adam's expression was one of utter surprise. "Sir?" he asked.

"Malcom is on the edge too. You know it. I know it. I need you
keep an eye on him for me, Adam. I gave him my word he would

make it home from this one. I can see in your eyes how much you still hurt from losing Julie."

Adam's lips twitched at the mention of his dead wife's name, but Brannon carefully pressed on.

"How do you think Malcom's wife and kids are gonna feel if he doesn't come home?"

Adam's expression became one of determination. "Ain't nobody deserves to lose the folks they love, Colonel. If you need me to babysit that pansy, I'll do it … for those he left in the States."

Brannon grinned. "Good. See? I knew I could count on you, Adam."

"Won't let you down, Colonel. That jerk will make it home. I'll see to that. You got nothing to worry about."

****

"Contact!" Sonar Tech Andy Carter shouted. "CBDR and closing fast!"

"It's the squid." Franklin looked to Captain Wall.

"Nothing else it could be," she agreed. "Evasive maneuvers! I don't want that thing plowing into us like it did the *Blackthorn.*"

Wall knew they couldn't really dodge the squid if ramming them was its intent. The thing was too fast, but she had given the order anyway.

"Take the squid with guns!" she added.

"Torpedoes away!" her weapons officer shouted. "Second volley ready in the tubes."

"Fire!" Wall shouted. "And keep firing!"

"Torpedoes closing on target," Carter called out then added excitedly. "Direct hits! Contact is changing course!"

"We've seen that before," Franklin commented.

Colonel Jackson was absent from the bridge. Wall wished he was here and for more reason than just her own nerves. Brannon noticed things that career navy officers might miss or overlook because of his inexperience with such things. She greatly valued that insight.

Brannon had assumed the task of getting everything ready for the crew of the *Nightstalker* to abandon ship when it got closer to the island. She had given him total command of what marines she had left aboard and any other seamen he needed to get the job done with.

"Don't remind me," Wall replied to her XO.

"Contact is coming about as expected!" Carter reported. "It's moved directly into our path and is inbound on an intercept heading."

"All weapons, fire!" Wall ordered.

Torpedoes launched from their tubes as the *Nightstalker*'s cannons opened up in their wake. A rain of death fell on the area of the water that the giant squid swam beneath. Wall prayed it would be enough. She figured she didn't have the firepower to kill the beast, unless she got luckier than she deserved to be, but she damn well wanted to bloody the thing and make it pay for the lives it had already taken from DESRON 44.

The sky had grown dark above the ship as the sun sunk below the distant horizon. The flashes of orange tracer rounds from the *Nightstalker*'s cannons flickered through the darkness as bright explosions blossomed ahead of her. Sprays of water splashed skyward as torpedoes struck their target beneath the waves. Wall hoped the water was black with the squid's oil-like blood.

The explosions grew louder and closer as the giant squid continued on its course straight towards a head-on collision with the *Nightstalker*. Surely that thing has to be hurting, Wall thought. Nothing could shrug off so many hits.

The squid was now too close for Wall's crew to use anything but the ship's cannons to strike at it. Bullets ripped into the water and Wall hoped they shredded the flesh they met there. This thing wasn't a fictional Godzilla, though it did seem nigh impossible to kill.

Wall grabbed hold of the arms of her command chair, hanging on with white knuckled determination as the *Nightstalker* lurched in the water. The squid had rammed into her but not with the force it had the *Blackthorn* earlier. Wall could tell from the sound of crunching metal that the ship had taken damage, but the *Nightstalker* had held together against the impact. She didn't know if it was because the squid was finally wounded to the point of being weakened or if it was simply because the *Nightstalker* was a far larger vessel than the *Blackthorn* had been. Wall started to yell for a damage report, but Franklin was already on it.

"We're taking on water!" he shouted at her. "Seventy-five percent of our forward weapon systems are offline including the CIWS."

"Causality report," Wall ordered.

"Twenty in the forward section known dead so far, more wounded. Reports are still coming in!"

"Ma'am!" Sonar Tech Carter shouted at her above the chaos that had taken over the bridge. "The contact is angling away. It appears to be headed out to swing around and build speed for another run at us."

"Keep firing at it with anything that still works!" Wall raged. "Odds are we won't survive a second hit like that one!"

Wall stabbed her personal comm. line. "Brannon, you better have those lifeboats loaded down and ready. We may need them sooner than expected!"

Wall closed the channel before Brannon could respond, returning her attention to the crisis she was dealing with. The squid had turned and was in route for the *Nightstalker* again. Her XO and crew were already doing all they could to slow the monster. The remaining functional deck cannons thundered and chattered, hosing the waves with a barrage of heavy fire. The forward torpedo launchers were lost and the aft ones useless with the creature coming in from the front. Wall slammed a fist into the arm of her chair in frustration. Nothing she and her crew did appeared to be enough. She felt helpless as Carter counted down the seconds to the next impact.

When it came, it brought death with it. The squid darted under the ship at the last second, its tentacles grasping upwards and around the *Nightstalker*. The metal of her hull whined and buckled under the creature's grip then gave in. Water poured inside the destroyer, flooding her lower levels. Wall listened to the cries of the men and women dying over the ship's intercom. Their desperate pleas for help tore at her very soul. There was nothing she could do for them though. She couldn't even help herself.

****

Over an hour had passed since the USS *Nightstalker* had been pulled downwards to a watery grave. Brannon sat on the beach of the island as the rest of the Reapers, except Vander and Zahn, worked to help the ship's other survivors unload the meager amount of gear they had been able to save. Only three of the smaller boats and life rafts Brannon had overseen getting into the water had reached the island's shore. There were fifteen people, *fifteen*, counting himself left alive from those aboard the *Nightstalker*. Zahn was missing. The Reapers had themselves up among the small crafter fleeing the sinking ship to ensure that some of them made it. Zahn hadn't. *Missing* was perhaps an overly generous label to the newbie's present state given the situation.

Brannon wasn't ready yet to admit that the kid was dead, so missing it would remain for the time being.

The night was dark but Adam, Malcom, and two crewmen from the *Nightstalker* had managed to get several fires going along the area of the beach where they came ashore. The fires were dangerous if there were still any of the smaller squid creatures on the island, but Brannon had allowed them anyway. With Vander on watch, they would see the things coming from a good distance out at the tree-line and have time to make a proper stand if it came to it.

It was going to be a long night. Brannon didn't dare lead the survivors into the island's jungle in the darkness. The squids, if they were still here, had enough advantages already. He needed time to get an inventory of what he had at hand. One thing was he knew for sure without even waiting on an inventory report from the others: They had no long-range comm. gear. He supposed it didn't matter, not with that giant monster out there emitting EM interference anyway. Brannon was sure the monster was hurting. He had gotten a glimpse of it as it rolled the *Nightstalker* in the water and took the ship down. The thing's body had been a mess of burnt, mangled, and bullet-peppered flesh. From the looks of it, the thing should have been dead but it wasn't. Somehow, it was continuing to hang on. Brannon wondered if squids regenerated. He knew certain types of lizards did. If the thing had such an ability, it would explain a good deal about why it wasn't rotting at the bottom of the ocean like by all rights it should be.

"Hey, Colonel!" Adam called to him. "Look what I found!"

Brannon broke away from his thoughts and looked over at Adam. The soldier was hoisting a minigun and waving it at him with a wide grin on his normally grim face.

"Did you find any ammo for it?" Brannon asked.

Adam nodded excitedly. "I call dibs on this baby."

"You got it." Brannon faked a smile.

Malcom approached Brannon as Adam went back to sorting through the gear being lugged from the lifeboats and took a seat on the sand next to him.

"You starting to believe me about just how screwed we are yet?"

Brannon did give a laugh then, a real one. "I never said I didn't believe you before."

"Could have fooled me with all that pep-talk-style crap you were throwing around." Malcom spat into the sand then suddenly got serious. "Look, I want you to know I don't blame you for this. Everybody's time comes someday and if this mess is mine, well, it's not like you held a gun to my head to get me to come."

"I did everything but that though," Brannon admitted. "I'm sorry, Malcom."

Malcom shrugged. "What's done is done I guess. I'll confess I was freaking out some back on the ship, but I think I've got it together now. Seeing all those hundreds of folks die as the *Nightstalker* went down sort of put things in perspective. There will be a lot of folks crying in the states when the word of what happened to their loved ones comes in."

"Assuming it gets declassified." Brannon matched Malcom's shrug with one of his own.

"Oh, they'll make up something I'm sure. It won't matter. Dead is dead no matter how you spin it."

"You got a point there," Brannon agreed. "Glad to see you're doing better too. Like I told you at the start, I need you on this one, Malcom."

"Dang straight you do." Malcom punched him in the shoulder. "Now you wanna tell me why I can't even go take a leak without Adam following me? I knew the guy was messed up, but I didn't think he had become a pervert too."

"That's my fault," Brannon chuckled, keeping his voice low. "I sort of asked him to keep an eye out for you. It's his job to make sure you see your family again."

Malcom gave a surprised grunt. "That's pretty sharp even for you. Two birds, one stone, and all that. Giving him a purpose may just be what he needs to hold it together. Guess that means I am going to have to endure him following me like a puppy, huh?"

Brannon nodded. "Until we get off this island at any rate."

"When was the last time you slept?"

"I could ask you the same."

"I'm not the one calling the shots, *sir*," Malcom said gruffly. "We need you sharp and you know it. Nothing you can do tonight anyway. You get some rest. I'll handle everything that needs doing until the sun comes up."

Brannon started to protest and then thought better of it. "Thanks," he said.

"I'll leave you to it then, boss," Malcom told him and got to his feet. "Trust me, I got this."

****

Brannon awoke to the rapid fire cracking of the M82 Vander had brought to the island with him this time. The high-powered, semi-auto weapon had a distinctive sound. Brannon rolled onto his feet, sweeping up his own M-16 in the process. His eyes scanned the beach around him, searching for the smaller squid creatures. There were none to be seen other than the mounds of splattered, black pulp Vander's fire had reduced the ones that had been near the tree-line to.

"Easy!" Malcom said, slipping up behind him. "Vander saw those things coming a good way out and just waited for them to be easier targets on the beach before dealing with them."

Brannon made a fist with his left hand, rubbing at his eyes. He held onto his rifle with his other as he collected himself. "Those were the only ones?"

"They're all we've seen so far."

"No sign of the big one? No doubt that thing has the reach to come after us on this beach," Brannon reminded Malcom.

Malcom shook his head. "No sign of that thing since it pulled the ship under. Thankfully, it's been a quiet night. Could it's too hurt to try or could be it's just leaving us alone because it sees us as food for any of its babies left alive here." Malcom paused and then gestured at a nearby fire. "Vander's got some coffee going if you want some."

Blinking in surprise, Brannon asked, "Vander has coffee? Are you serious?"

"Apparently, he carries his own stash with him. Offered to share some of it this morning. As weird as that kid is, I kind of like him today," Malcom laughed, lifting a metal mug at Brannon.

Brannon headed to the fire where the coffee was and removed a mug from a backpack of survival gear resting on the beach beside it. He poured himself half a cup and took a seat on the sand, staring into the crackling blaze of the fire. The weather was warm but not so hot as to make the heat of the fire too uncomfortable. He took a sip of the coffee and smiled at Malcom who had followed him.

"This stuff is pretty good," he admitted.

"You know Vander. Everything has to be the best of the best, even his rations," Malcom chuckled. "We moving out today?"

"Don't see how we have much of a choice," Brannon said. "We can't stay on this beach. The elements will get us even if the squids don't."

"You really think there are enough of those things left on this island to be a threat? I mean, the two destroyers of DESRON 44 ripped this place a new one. Just look at those trees up there."

Brannon glanced at the tree-line and saw what Malcom meant. Many of the trees were splintered, others blackened from fire. Nearly all of the undergrowth surrounding them was dead.

"We're playing it safe until we know for sure," Brannon answered.

"I'm all for doing that," Malcom agreed, "but if help comes, we'll be easier to spot out here."

"And if it doesn't?" Brannon asked.

Malcom had no answer.

"We know those cultists had facilities all over this place. Could be there are some, maybe even underground ones, that survived what DESRON 44 did to this place."

"Wouldn't count on it," Malcom snorted.

"Even so, finding one would make all our lives a lot easier until help does come and any kind of real structure will be a lot safer than just sitting around out here." Brannon gestured up and down the beach.

Brannon slugged down what was left of his coffee and got up. "How are the survivors from the *Nightstalker*'s crew holding up?"

"Varies." Malcom frowned. "Most of them are the marines that were helping us load up the gear, but we got ourselves a cook, a sonar tech, and an engineering mate too."

"Always has to be a cook and never one like Seagal."

"I hate Seagal. Never seen a movie I liked with him in it." Malcom shook his head.

"Me too, but you have to admit, a cook that can fight is better than a guy who went through basic years ago and has spent his days frying eggs."

"Guess so," Malcom half-heartedly agreed.

Malcom's expression shifted suddenly as if he was just remembering something that needed to be said. "Oh, and boss, the sonar tech, it's that Andy guy."

"Carter from the bridge?" Brannon blurted as it hit him that Wall had to be dead. "How in the devil did he make it out?"

"No idea, but you can ask him if you want."

"I think I just might … when we get time for things like that," Brannon said. "Right now, we need to get our gear up and our butts moving. This daylight isn't going to last forever and we'll need to find somewhere to hole up before night falls. Are the helmet comms. still working?"

Malcom nodded.

"Then send Vander on ahead. He can handle himself out there and works better alone anyhow. Tell Adam he's on point. You'll be bringing up the rear. I want a Reaper back there with eyes I can trust."

"Yes, sir," Malcom saluted and then rushed away to get the survivors of DESRON 44 geared up and moving into the jungle.

****

Vander was long gone by the time the other Reapers and the surviving folks from the *Nightstalker* got moving. Adam was on point, his minigun ready. Brannon walked with the marines that made up the column's middle. Some patches of the jungle were burnt to the ground and were nothing more than blackened clearings of ash. The rest though was just as Brannon remembered it. Brannon kept his eyes on the trees. If the squids attacked, they would almost certainly use them. They traveled much faster swinging through the tree tops than they did on foot or club or whatever the heck you called it. When the squids walked, they reminded him for the tripods from H.G. Wells' War of the Worlds, only they were supported solely by two long tentacles that ended in hooked clubs. He would have never believed how fast the squids could move in such a fashion had he not seen it himself. The strength of their two main tentacles was staggering to behold. He remembered the torn metal he had seen inside the cultists' compound and shuddered as a chill passed through him despite the heat of the sun.

He hadn't sent Vander on ahead to warn the group of any squids that might be waiting on them in what was left of the jungle. Brannon had sent the sniper on to find them shelter. Vander would be able to move faster alone and was more than able to take care of himself. If they found shelter, it would likely be because of him. As a sniper, Vander was much more in touch with his surroundings than anyone else in the group. He was likely to spot something the rest of them might very well overlook.

Brannon noticed a squid hanging from a tree not too far ahead of the column. Adam had seen it too and motioned for everyone to stop. Brannon moved to join Adam on point.

"One of them things is up there, Colonel." Adam gestured at the creature with the barrels of his minigun.

"One isn't a problem," Brannon assured him. "We just need to figure out some way to take it out quietly."

Adam snorted. "Don't see that happening, sir."

Brannon sighed. "Yeah, to tell the truth, I don't either."

"We could go around it, give it a wide berth. That would lower the odds of it coming after us alone."

Brannon shook his head. "We leave this trail and we're screwed. Going around it would put us deeper in the trees."

"Beginning to regret you sent Vander on ahead? I'll bet my left foot he's got a silencer on him somewhere."

Brannon smiled. "We need Vander out there. I'll deal with the squid."

Bracing the butt of his M-16 against his shoulder, Brannon raised the weapon and took aim at the squid. He knew he needed to pull off the whole "one shot, one kill" thing that snipers always went on about. The problem was that he was shooting a creature that he didn't even really know where its major organs were, not another human being. He aimed carefully for the thing's central body mass and hoped that single three-round burst there would do the trick.

Brannon was about to squeeze the trigger when gunfire erupted from the rear of the column. The squid he was aiming for started moving. Brannon took his shot, but the squid was too fast. His rounds dug into the tree where the squid had been hanging as it propelled itself forward. It came, flying through the air, at him. The barrels of Adam's minigun spun, turning the squid into little more than a red mist before it ever hit the ground.

"Thanks." Brannon nodded at Adam. Adam gave a shrug as the two of them turned to see Malcom and the marines from the *Nightstalker* engaged with a group of squids attacking the rear of the column. They were professionals, quickly spreading out and establishing a wide field of fire. The cook was carrying a pump-action shotgun and held back with Andy behind the marines' pincer formation. Andy was clutching the M-16 he carried in a white-knuckled grip as Brannon reached him.

"You know how to use that?" Brannon shouted over the gunfire.

Andy shook his head in the negative. "It won't fire."

Brannon reached over and flicked off the weapon's safety. "I suggest you learn fast."

Adam charged into the center of the marines, adding his fire to theirs. The barrels of his minigun spun as he belted out a war cry, holding down its trigger. Adam swept the stream of fire from the minigun over the mass of squids swinging through the trees. Squids died by the dozens, their torn and mangled bodies dropping to the jungle floor.

"Fire in the hole!" one of the marines shouted, lobbing a grenade into the trees. The explosion did little to the squids still in the trees, but it blew apart of several of the ones who were scrambling along on their two primary tentacles towards the marines' position.

"Sir!" one of the marines called to him as Brannon put a burst of rounds into a squid that was mid-leap between tree limbs. The thing's body flopped to the ground leaking black blood and lay there twitching, its tentacles whipping about wildly.

"We can't keep this up, sir!" the marine told him. "We don't have the ammo for this kind of prolonged engagement!"

Brannon knew the man was right, but what the devil was he supposed to do about it? It was taking everything they had just to keep the squids pushed back. If they tried to disengage and run, the squids would tear them apart.

At that moment, Adam's minigun clicked empty. Brannon was surprised its ammo had lasted as long as it did. The difference the weapon had made became clear in a heartbeat. Without its sweeping fire to keep the bulk of the squids at bay, the creatures came, hurling themselves into the marines' lines. One marine howled in pain as a squid impaled him with one its primary tentacles as it leaped from a tree onto him. Its other tentacles wrapped about his body like snakes, constricting to the sound of cracking bones folding inward.

Another marine had a squid drop directly onto him from a tree. Its tentacles spread over him in a dome shape as its mouth landed in a perfect position to rip into his skull. The marine collapsed with the squid on top of him, its beak-like mouth covered in brain matter. Brannon killed the thing with a quick burst, but the marine was long dead. He had died the instance his skull had been cracked open like an egg.

"Fall back!" Brannon yelled, trying to lay down what cover fire he could for the remaining marines, but it seemed useless. Instead of shrinking from the losses the squid had taken, the number of squids had tripled in the last thirty seconds.

Brannon watched one marine turn to run. The man looked like he was going to make it until a squid hurled itself from a tree limb onto his back. Its two main tentacles snaked around his torso as its lesser ones slashed and stabbed at him. Two of the smaller tentacles ripped most of the flesh from the marine's face in an instant as the other ones stabbed into him over and over again like living knives. The marine's blood sprayed outward in wet splashes of red. His screams were suddenly silenced as a tentacle plunged into his mouth. Brannon saw its tip emerge through the marine's right eye socket. It writhed about above where the marine's eye dangled against the jagged and ripped meat of his cheek, held on by the thinnest strand of sinew. Brannon jerked his eyes away from the grizzly scene as a squid threw itself at him.

Twisting his body about, Brannon barely managed to dodge the squid's attack. It landed on the ground beside him and rose up on its two primary tentacles to tower over him. Brannon stared at the monster, his mouth hanging open. He had never seen one of the ground squids as large as it before. A shotgun thundered and its black blood exploded onto him. Brannon felt a hand grab him and roughly drag him away from the squid's collapsing form. The cook had saved his life.

Brannon didn't need to be told to run. His legs pumped under him as he followed the cook northward along the trail. Brannon glanced over his shoulder to see why the squids hadn't overtaken them already. He saw Adam standing in the middle of the trail, an M-16 in each hand, blazing away at the monsters. Malcom was at his side, his own M-16 spitting carefully aimed, three-round bursts that sent a squid to Hell every time he fired. The two Reapers were at home in the center of such bloodshed and Brannon knew he would never see either of them again.

****

Brannon, the cook, and the last three marines ran for what felt like an eternity. When they finally stopped, night was falling over the island. Shadows grew longer in the dying rays of the setting sun. Brannon leaned against a tree, panting and fighting for breath. The cook had collapsed onto the jungle floor and lay there unmoving, his entire body dripping with sweat. The marines were exhausted too, but they kept their weapons ready and their eyes scanning the tree tops as they caught what rest they could.

Andy was gone. Brannon would never have the chance to ask the sonar tech how he had survived the sinking of the *Nightstalker* or about Captain Wall's final moments. That bothered Brannon, but nowhere near as much as the loss of Malcom and Adam. Their loss was burning pain in his heart that left him feeling lost and defeated. They had both been friends and good men. It wasn't right that they had died like they had. He knew there would be no point in returning for their bodies later even if he was able to. The squids would have devoured their corpses down to the bones.

"Colonel," one of the marines named Chris said, "I think the cook is dead."

Brannon blinked in surprise. He looked down at the cook where he lay and noticed the man didn't appear to be breathing. Brannon leaped to kneel beside the cook and checked for a pulse. He couldn't find one.

"Heart attack?" a marine named Joe put forth as an explanation.

"Had to be," Beck, the last marine, agreed.

"Damn it all to hell." Brannon wept over the cook's corpse. "One of you make sure to take his shotgun when we start moving again. We're going to need it."

Crackled filled Brannon's ear as his comm. helmet came to life. "Colonel? You there?"

"Vander!" Brannon shouted, ignoring the odd looks from the marines around him. "You're alive!"

"Uh, why wouldn't I be, boss?" Vander asked, stunned by Brannon's excitement.

"We were attacked. Malcom and Adam are dead, along with the majority of the others."

"Malcom *and* Adam?" Vander's voice grew even colder than it usually sounded.

Brannon nodded though he knew Vander couldn't see it. "Both of them," he confirmed. "They went out together in a blaze of glory."

"Figures they would go out like that," Vander commented, his voice devoid of emotion. "Look, boss, I've found something. Let me give you the coordinates."

Brannon listened to Vander, memorizing everything he could that the sniper told him then turned back to the three marines who were staring at him, grinning like a lunatic.

"Good news, Colonel?" Chris asked.

"Vander's found us somewhere to hole up until help arrives. It's not far either."

"Then what the heck are we waiting for?" Joe urged him.

Brannon led the marines through the trees as the darkness grew thicker in the trees. They appeared to have lost the squids at least for the time being. Brannon knew they owed Adam and Malcom for that.

The place Vander had found was an underground bunker of some type. Its entrance was concealed by vines and Brannon knew he never would have found it without Vander's instructions. He shoved the vines aside and slammed the butt of his rifle against the metal of the door behind them.

Light spilled out from the entrance as Vander opened the door to let Brannon and others inside. Vander closed the entrance behind them.

"Welcome to the creepiest place on earth, Colonel," Vander chuckled coldly.

"The power's on here?" Brannon asked, shocked. With how hard the destroyers of DESRON 44 had pounded the island, he wouldn't have believed that would have been possible.

"Oh yeah," Vander nodded, "and that's just the tip of the iceberg so to speak. Follow me."

The entrance corridor opened into a vast, underground base. It was a wide, open structure that resembled the inside of a warehouse. There were crates scattered everywhere. Their labels were in a language that Brannon didn't even recognize. There were two computer stations as well.

"What is all this?" Brannon asked Vander.

"I think this was supposed to be the cultists' version of a panic room. Clearly, none of them made it here though. No idea what language that is on those crates, but I've opened a few. Some are loaded with ammo and others food stuffs. There's running water, showers, and toilets at the rear of the room even."

"And those?" Brannon gestured at the two computer stations.

"Those are where things really start to get interesting." Vander smiled. In addition to being the Reapers' sniper, he was also the squad's computer expert and hacker. "One is a surveillance setup. You can pull up images from all over the island on it. The other is, from what I can tell so far, a backup data storage unit and server for the work the cultists were doing here."

It took a moment for what Vander was saying to sink in before Brannon grabbed Vander by his shoulders. "Can you use it to contact DESRON 12?"

"Given time, I think I can." Vander smiled. "We just might live through this one after all, boss."

****

Brannon and the marines settled in as Vander worked at the cultists' computer station. The bunker was air conditioned and it was a pleasant change from being out in the elements of the island. Chris and Joe dug into the case of rations that Vander had opened and whipped up a meal in the tiny kitchen area that adjoined the main room of the bunker. Beck hadn't emerged from the showers yet. The marine was taking his time back there. Brannon had taken an extended shower himself. The blood of the squids was a thick, crude oil-type substance and not easy to clean off. Brannon had used the shower to wash his clothes as best he could too. They were still dripping wet when he put them back on. He felt much better after his shower and the temperature in bunker was comfortable, so he didn't mind the wetness covering his body. In a sense, it was refreshing, and let him know he was alive.

He and the marines had opened several others of the scattered crates. Some contained AK-47s. He and the marines had traded out their M-16s from the weapons. There was plenty of ammo in the bunker for the AKs where as they were almost out of rounds for the M-16s. Brannon was a fan of the AK-47 anyway. He blamed it on his dad making him watch the A-Team when he was younger. Regardless, the AK-47 he had picked felt good in his hands. He made sure it was loaded and strapped with several magazines for the weapon onto his combat suit before he joined Chris and Joe for the meal that has assembled. It was mostly rice and fish, but he was glad to have it. He couldn't remember the last time he had eaten and his body needed the calories. He wolfed down one mouthful of fish and rice after another until his stomach didn't have room for anymore.

"Thanks," he told Chris and Joe before he got up and left them to check on Vander's progress.

"Any luck?" Brannon asked.

"Yes and no." Vander frowned. "If you mean contacting DESRON 12, not yet, but I've found crap you won't believe in the cultists' files."

"Do tell," Brannon urged him.

"The files you pulled from their compound weren't complete. Everything we've thought we knew about these squids and where they come from is a load of crap. We thought they never found their 'god' they were looking for but they did. It was really asleep on the ocean floor here."

"The giant squid," Brannon said aloud.

Vander grimaced. "Exactly. I don't believe that thing is a god any more than you do. My best guess is that it's something left over from an age long before man walked the earth. Maybe it's some kind of mutant. Whatever it is, they harvested its DNA to create the smaller version of it we've been fighting here. Despite their claims of wanting to wake it up, the cultists left it slumbering. Everything was going awesome for them until it did wake."

Brannon was hanging on Vander's every word and trying hard to make sense of it all.

"When it did wake up, that's when things took a dark turn for our cultist buddies. The smaller creatures they had been creating turned on them. Something took control of them, AKA the giant one out there that destroyed DESRON 44. The cultists put up a good fight, but as you know, it wasn't enough."

"Anything in there about how to stop those things?"

"Nada," Vander said sadly. "The cultists didn't have any failsafe in place. I think they really believed they could control the squids and use them as weapons against the rest of the world. Who knows? They very well might have too if the big one hadn't woken up. All of the ones from the initial batch of smaller squids that they created had chips in them that were connected to their nervous systems. The tech is really impressive and beyond anything I've seen before. Of course, I'm a computer geek not a biologist, but clearly it worked to a degree at first. The cultists could send simple, limited commands to the smaller squids and the creature would obey them."

"Wow," Brannon muttered.

"Wow is right," Vander agreed. "The big one ... I can't tell you how it controls or communicates with the smaller ones, but I can tell you it does on both counts. I can also tell you, based on the data about the tissue samples the cultists extracted from it, that it does regenerate too. The only hope of ever killing it is to do in one single shot that does so much damage to the thing that it just shuts down."

"Then why don't the little ones heal like that if they were created from it?" Brannon asked.

Vander shrugged. "The DNA the cultists used either mutated when they used it or was intentionally changed. You're right though. The little ones don't heal any faster than a normal squid. Instead, their reproductive rate is through the roof. Whether the cultists knew what they were doing or not, they did create monsters with the potential to wipe out the human race. Captain Wall was right when she decided to frag this place. Trouble is, it's going to take a lot more than the firepower of two destroyers to do it. I'm not even sure a nuke would work now. The smaller squids have spread into the ocean so only God knows how many of them there are now or how far they've extended themselves beyond the island."

"Dear God," Brannon rasped. "Are we really talking about the end of the world?"

"I think so, boss." Vander nodded. "Unless we stop them right *now*. Could be I was wrong about us making it home, Colonel. I'm sorry."

Brannon's exhaustion was beginning to catch up to him despite Vander's news. He rubbed at his eyes. "We'll see," Brannon said, trying not to sound like he had given up hope too. "I need to get some sleep before my brain completely shuts down on its own."

"Wait," Vander stopped him. "There's one more thing."

Brannon wondered what other bad news Vander could possibly have left to give him.

"I said the cultists didn't have a failsafe against the squids, but guess what the power source for all their equipment on this island is?"

"What?" Brannon asked, beginning to get annoyed.

"It's all nuclear, Colonel. There's a reactor at the center of the island, a really, really big one."

Brannon stared at Vander. "You don't mean…"

"Yep. If we blow it, Colonel, we might have a chance at killing all the squids if they haven't spread too far yet."

"So much for going home," Brannon said, putting his hands over his face and running them along the curves of his cheeks. Then Brannon asked, "Wait. I thought you couldn't really blow up a nuclear reactor like what you're talking about."

"Normally, you would be right," Vander smiled, "but these were lunatic cultists we're talking about who built the thing. They rigged it, weaponized it somehow, according to the data in this thing. If we can trigger it, it'll set off a blast on the level of a fifty megaton explosion."

Brannon stared at Vander in disbelief. "What about the environmental damage?"

"Compared to an unending army of man-eating squids? You're joking right?"

Brannon didn't know how to respond.

"We *need* to do it," Vander pressed him. "Otherwise, the folks back home will have a war on their hands they won't even see coming."

"I know," Brannon assured him. "You find out where the reactor is and how to blow it. I'll tell the others in the morning.

This bunker is secure. Ain't nothing getting through that entrance door. Let the others get one last good night's sleep at least."

"The longer we wait…"

"Four hours, Vander. Give them that much. We all need it, even you. As soon as you find out what we need to know, I want you to grab as much sleep as you can too. Tomorrow, we have to save the world."

****

The marines didn't take the news well over breakfast. Finding out the meal you're eating will be your last one is not something anyone wants to wake up to. It was the truth though. His mind clearer now from the rest he had gotten, Brannon was certain blowing the reactor at the center of the island was the course they had to take. Saving the world wasn't all the awesome it was cracked up to be when you had to die to do it. It was cold comfort to know that so many others would live. No matter how noble the act of accepting one's own death as the cost of it is, it's a hard thing for most human beings to do.

Brannon counted himself lucky that he didn't have any family to speak of alive outside of Vander. Even the rest of his Reapers were dead. The marine, Chris, wasn't so lucky. He had daughters at home. Like any dad, his girls were his world. Brannon didn't doubt that Chris would help get the job done because of them too, but with the loss of Adam and Malcom so fresh for him, he could imagine how Chris felt at the thought of never seeing them again.

Vander had mapped out the shortest and most direct route from the bunker to the cultists' main compound. Even so, they still had to travel a solid two miles on foot through the jungle. Vander claimed the squids were less active during the daylight hours than at night, but all of them knew that even if that was the case, the number of squids might be less, but it would still be more than enough to wipe them out easily. They had all fought the squids during the day before.

The only good news that Vander had to share was that he had managed to hack into the cultists' system that controlled the original batches of squids they had created. Vander had not only managed to hack his way in but also had, he believed, taken control of those squids, reprogramming the creatures. He had changed their biological directives to attack the other, later-born squids. *That* would certainly help if there were any of those squids still alive.

Brannon, Vander, and the three marines gathered at the bunker's door. All of them were armed to the teeth, carrying as many weapons and as much ammo as they could. Even if Vander's reprogramming of the original squids had worked, it was going to be a running battle all the way to the cultists' compound and they all knew it.

"You ready?" Brannon asked.

"No," Vander said and keyed the code that opened the thick metal door in front of them. It slid open to let in the sunlight of the day outside.

Brannon led the charge, bursting out into the jungle, as the others followed.

****

Almost immediately, the high-pitched, squeal-like shrieks of the squids arose in the distant trees. Brannon did his best to ignore them, focusing his attention solely on the trees he ran underneath.

"They're coming!" Vander shouted.

Several squids appeared ahead of the group, swinging through the trees from one limb to another with their two primary tentacles. The creatures moved like lightning. Chris paused to open fire on them and died where he stood. A squid came swinging through the trees to his right and hurled itself onto the marine. Chris tried to jerk the barrel of his M-16 around to meet it but was too slow. One of the squid's lesser tentacles wrapped around the weapon and yanked it from his hands. Chris was frantically trying to claw his sidearm from its holster when the squid struck him. The impact knocked him off his feet. He toppled to the ground with the squid writhing on top of him. Several of the creature's tentacles dug into his flesh like burrowing worms. Chris screamed as they worked their way through his guts inside him.

Joe slowed on the verge of turning around to help Chris.

"Keep moving!" Brannon heard Vander yell at the marine, but the warning came too late.

A squid landed on the ground next to Joe. One of its tentacles shot out, tearing into his back. The tentacle ripped Joe's spinal column from his body with a single, fierce tug.

Brannon, Vander, and Beck kept moving. They picked up their speed, pushing their bodies to their limits. If they slowed down or tried to stand and fight, they were dead and they knew it.

As the compound or rather what was left of it came into view, the squids were all around them. Brannon heard Beck scream. The marine vanished beneath a mass of squids that caught up to him and swarmed him. Beck's screams changed to horrid, gargling noises as the creatures tore him apart and quickly fell silent.

"There!" Vander shouted, pointing at a sealed hatch which appeared to lead underground amid the wreckage of the compound. Brannon reached it and flung it open. Vander dived head first through it. Brannon tried to follow, but a tentacle snagged his ankle as he made the jump. He dangled inside the short shaft into the compound's underground interior. A single bullet from Vander's M82 severed the tentacle holding him and Brannon screamed as he fell towards where Vander waited below.

****

Brannon woke up with an aching head. . It felt as if an ape had gone wild on his skull with a metal pipe. It took a moment for his vision to come into focus. When it did, he saw he was in a small, enclosed room. He wasn't alone. Vander stood at a computer station on the far side of the room, the sniper's fingers dancing hurriedly over its control keys. Vander must have noticed that he was awake.

"Didn't know if you were going to make it or not, Colonel," Vander commented not taking his eyes off the work he was doing.

"We made it?" Brannon asked not sure where they were.

"We made it," Vander told him. "This room we're in is the control room for the island's reactor."

"What happened?" Brannon gently touched his forehead. His fingers came away slicked red.

"You mean after you fell down that shaft onto your head?" Vander laughed. "I dragged your butt into the closest corridor and got it sealed before the squids were able to reach us."

"Thanks," Brannon said.

"Don't thank me," Vander said. "We're still dead. The doors between us and the squids aren't strong enough to hold them. They've torn through quite a few while you were out. I've been watching them on the security monitor over there."

Brannon turned his head and for the first time noticed the screen Vander was talking about it.

"As soon as I cracked the computer in here, I set it to follow the squids' movement through the base so I would know how much time I had left to finish up here."

"How long?" Brannon got to his feet, glad to see his AK-47 was propped against the wall near where he had been lying.

"Not long enough," Vander said grimly. "At the rate those things are tearing through this base, they'll be here in less than five minutes. I need at least eight to finish the breaking the code that will make the reactor blow. You feel like being a hero one last time?"

"As if I had a choice," Brannon growled. "You say you need eight minutes?"

"Total, at least," Vander answered. "If you can buy me a few more, I'll take them. I've got a few prayers I need to say."

"I didn't know you believed in God."

"Why? Because I'm a geek?" Vander laughed. "Oh, I believe in Jesus and I know where I'm going when we get this done, Colonel. You can count on that. Hope you do too."

Brannon checked the magazine in his AK-47 and made sure he had more magazines within easy reach on his belt. "Ten minutes then," he said.

"Just make sure you close the doors behind you as you go out to meet those things, Colonel. Every second counts and those doors will slow them some."

"You got it," Brannon said. "Vander, I just want you to know…"

"Don't," Vander told him. "Just get the job done. I'll see you again on the other side, Colonel."

Brannon gave Vander a sharp nod and headed out through the twisting corridors of the compound to meet the approaching squids.

****

Brannon made his way through the compound until he came to a door where he heard the squids on its other side. Hammering blows rang out as the squids slammed the clubs of their primary tentacles into it. The hooks of those clubs dug into the metal of the door, piercing it, as the squids strained to pull the door from the walls holding it in place. With each passing second, the door grew weaker. Brannon positioned himself a good distance away from the door and rechecked his AK-47.

The door was jerked towards the squids as they finally tore it free of the walls. It clanged to the floor of the corridor as the squids swarmed around its falling mass. They came along the floor, the sides of the wall, and even running across the ceiling of the corridor. The whole corridor was filled with a tidal wave of swarming squids. Brannon fired into the mass of creatures on full auto, emptying his first magazine. Before he ejected the spent mag. to ram a fresh one home, he lobbed a grenade at the squids to buy himself some time. The explosion rocked the corridor. Black blood and pieces of charred, mangled squid flesh flew everywhere. Still, the squids came on.

Brannon retreated through the doorway behind him, closing it, and repeating the same process with each doorway until he found himself only one away from where Vander was working. He checked his watch as the squids went to work on breaking through the last door he had sealed. He had bought Vander seven minutes so far, but he was out of places to run and down to his last magazine. He had no grenades to throw this time. He watched each second tick by until they broke into the section of corridor he stood in.

Opening fire, Brannon held the trigger of his AK-47 tight. Bullets flew from its barrel, cutting the squids at the head of the mass of creature to shreds. It wasn't his fire but the bodies of their own dead that slowed the squids just as it had been at each doorway during his fighting retreat.

When his magazine ran out, Brannon threw his AK-47 towards the squids, drawing the pistol holstered on his hip. He brought it up in a two-handed grip, getting off three, well-placed shots that ripped into the central mass of the lead squid. It shrieked as it died before its corpse was swept aside by the squids behind it.

Brannon didn't even have time to scream when the wave of squids struck him. He felt his arms and legs pulled away from his body before a thick tentacle buried itself in his forehead and his world went dark.

****

Vander heard the door behind him give way. Squids came pouring into the reactor's control room. He turned to meet them with a smile, puffing on a cigarette.

"About time, you bastards," he laughed before the room was filled with a white flash of heat that burnt Vander and the squids away into nothingness.

Epilogue

The destroyers of DESRON 12 were state-of-the-art and shielded against EMP. Despite that shielding, the EMP that washed over them was so powerful, their lights flickered before going out and their systems crashed. It took several minutes for things to come back online. Surface community captain Peter Romero stood on the bridge of the USS *Laybourne* surrounded by chaos. His crew was working hard to make sure all the ships of DESRON 12 hadn't taken any serious damage from the effects of the EMP. Romero's people were telling him that the blast which caused the EMP had to be well over ten megatons in nature. They had no explanation for where such a blast could have come from or who would have detonated such a device. Romero had been fully briefed on DESRON 44's mission and the island of cultists they were dispatched to deal with. Still, he found it difficult to believe the cultists could have had such a weapon at their disposal.

DESRON 44 was presumed lost at the center of the blast, which generated the EMP that struck the ships of his own DESRON, was the island the cultists were, or rather, had been based on. Romero hadn't known Captain Wall or Colonel Jackson well, but he knew their reps. They were both among the best of the best. All he could figure was that the cultists had been left with no choice but to use the "doomsday" weapon that intel said they were working on rather than lose it.

"Sir!" Henderson, his sonar tech, shouted at him. "We've got surface contacts CRDB at a speed of twenty-five knots. ETA in five!"

"Friendlies?" Captain Romero asked.

"They're not answering hails and I'm not picking up any transponder signals either," his comm. officer reported.

"Whoever they are, Captain, there are a lot of them," Henderson told him.

The day just kept getting stranger and stranger, Romero thought. Someone out there in the direction the contacts were approaching from had just detonated a large-scale nuclear weapon, so he wasn't willing to risk taking any chances.

"Prepare to take the contacts with guns!" Romero ordered.

"Sir!" Henderson shouted. "More contacts have just *appeared* around the *Hyatt* and the *Lifeson!*"

"What do you mean appeared?" Romero snapped.

Before Henderson could respond, the comm. officer interrupted them. "Captain!" she yelled. "The *Hyatt* and *Lifeson* are reporting they are under attack and being boarded."

"Boarded?" Romero repeated the word in utter disbelief. "Who's attacking them?"

His comm. officer's expression was one of confusion edged with terror as she answered, "They claim to be under attack by squids, sir. Squids are emerging from the water and scaling the sides of their ships."

"Action stations!" Romero ordered his crew. "Scramble our rapid response teams! I want this ship ready if the same happens to us!"

"Original contacts still on screen and approaching, Captain," Henderson reminded him.

"Blow them out of the water," he growled at his weapon's officer before taking a seat in his command chair. Romero's mind was reeling from the insanity of what he was facing, but he damned sure wasn't going to let some bloody squids overrun DESRON 12. Not on his watch.

Eric S. Brown is author of numerous series including the Bigfoot War series, the Crypto-Squad series (with Jason Brannon), the Kaiju Apocalypse series (with Jason Cordova), The Homeworld series, The "A Pack of Wolves" series, and the Jack Bunny Bam-Bam series. Some of his stand alone books include Kraken, Megalodon, Megalodons, Megalodon Apocalypse, War of the World Plus Blood Guts and Zombies, Sasquatch Lake, Crawlers, Season of Rot, and Kaiju Armageddon to name only a few. His short fiction has been published hundreds of times in the small press and beyond including markets like Baen Books' Onward Drake and Black Tide Rising anthologies, the Grantville Gazette, Walmart Wolrd Magazine, and the SNAFU anthology series. He has written the novelizations for such films as Boggy Creek: The Legend is True and The Bloody Rage of Bigfoot. Two of his own books have been adapted into feature films the first of which was Bigfoot War in 2014 by Origin Releasing. Eric also writes an ongoing comic book news column entitled "Comics in a Flash." He lives in North Carolina with his wife and two children where he continues to write tales of blazing guns, hungry corpses, and the monsters that lurk in the woods.

CHECK OUT OTHER GREAT DEEP SEA THRILLERS

THEY RISE
by Hunter Shea

Some call them ghost sharks, the oldest and strangest looking creatures in the sea.

Marine biologist Brad Whitley has studied chimaera fish all his life. He thought he knew everything about them. He was wrong. Warming ocean temperatures free legions of prehistoric chimaera fish from their methane ice suspended animation. Now, in a corner of the Bermuda Triangle, the ocean waters run red. The 400 million year old massive killing machines know no mercy, destroying everything in their path. It will take Whitley, his climatologist ex-wife and the entire US Navy to stop them in the bloodiest battle ever seen on the high seas.

SERPENTINE
by Barry Napier

Clarkton Lake is a picturesque vacation spot located in rural Virginia, great for fishing, skiing, and wasting summer days away.

But this summer, something is different. When butchered bodies are discovered in the water and along the muddy banks of Clarkton Lake, what starts out as a typical summer on the lake quickly turns into a nightmare.

This summer, something new lives in the lake...something that was born in the darkest depths of the ocean and accidentally brought to these typically peaceful waters.

It's getting bigger, it's getting smarter...and it's always hungry.

CHECK OUT OTHER GREAT DEEP SEA THRILLERS

SEA RAPTOR
by John J. Rust

From terrorist hunter to monster hunter! Jack Rastun was a decorated U.S. Army Ranger, until an unfortunate incident forced him out of the service. He is soon hired by the Foundation for Undocumented Biological Investigation and given a new mission, to search for cryptids, creatures whose existence has not been proven by mainstream science. Teaming up with the daring and beautiful wildlife photographer Karen Thatcher, they must stop a sea monster's deadly rampage along the Jersey Shore. But that's not the only danger Rastun faces. A group of murderous animal smugglers also want the creature. Rastun must utilize every skill learned from years of fighting, otherwise, his first mission for the FUBI might very well be his last.

OCEAN'S HAMMER
by D.J. Goodman

Something strange is happening in the Sea of Cortez. Whales are beaching for no apparent reason and the local hammerhead shark population, previously believed to be fished to extinction, has suddenly reappeared. Marine biologists Maria Quintero and Kevin Hoyt have come to investigate with a television producer in tow, hoping to get footage that will land them a reality TV show. The plan is to have a stand-off against a notorious illegal shark-fishing captain and then go home.

Things are not going according to plan.

There is something new in the waters of the Sea of Cortez. Something smart. Something huge. Something that has its own plans for Quintero and Hoyt.

CHECK OUT OTHER GREAT
DEEP SEA THRILLERS

MEGATOOTH
by Viktor Zarkov

When the death rate of sperm whales rises dramatically, a well-respected environmental activist puts together a ragtag team to hit the high seas to investigate the matter. They suspect that the deaths are due to poachers and they are all driven by a need for justice.

Elsewhere, an experimental government vessel is enhancing deep sea mining equipment. They see one of these dead whales up close and personal...and are fairly certain that it wasn't poachers that killed it.

Both of these teams are about to discover that poachers are the least of their worries. There is something hunting the whales...

Something big
Something prehistoric.
Something terrifying.
MEGATOOTH!

BLOOD CRUISE
by Jake Bible

Ben Clow's plans are set. Drop off kids, pick up girlfriend, head to the marina, and hop on best friend's cruiser for a weekend of fun at sea. But Ben's happy plans are about to be changed by a tentacled horror that lurks beneath the waves.

International crime lords! Deep cover black ops agents! A ravenous, bloodsucking monster! A storm of evil and danger conspire to turn Ben Clow's vacation from a fun ocean getaway into a nightmare of a Blood Cruise!

CHECK OUT OTHER GREAT
DEEP SEA THRILLERS

PREDATOR X
by C.J Waller

When deep level oil fracking uncovers a vast subterranean sea, a crack team of cavers and scientists are sent down to investigate. Upon their arrival, they disappear without a trace. A second team, including sedimentologist Dr Megan Stoker, are ordered to seek out Alpha Team and report back their findings. But Alpha team are nowhere to be found – instead, they are faced with something unexpected in the depths. Something ancient. Something huge. Something dangerous. Predator X

DEAD BAIT
by Tim Curran

A husband hell-bent on revenge hunts a Wereshark...A Russian mail order bride with a fishy secret...Crabs with a collective consciousness...A vampire who transforms into a Candiru...Zombie piranha...Bait that will have you crawling out of your skin and more. Drawing on horror, humor with a helping of dark fantasy and a touch of deviance, these 19 contemporary stories pay homage to the monsters that lurk in the murky waters of our imaginations. If you thought it was safe to go back in the water...Think Again!

www.ingramcontent.com/pod-product-compliance
Lightning Source LLC
Chambersburg PA
CBHW030537130626
46552CB00006B/2305